From bad to worse . . .

As soon as the first bell rang, I left that room and walked into the corridor, ready to burst into tears. Keeping my head down, I rushed through the crowded hall toward the bathroom.

In my watery-eyed haze I saw Jessica and Elizabeth walking toward me. I faked a smile in their direction and headed into the girls' room, then stood still and took a few deep breaths. Looking in the mirror, I tried to give myself a pep talk.

"Get ahold of yourself, Kristin," I said softly. "Don't let them get to you. You're class president, and you're going to show the class council that you're a good leader and that your ideas are good ones." I nodded firmly, then tried to even out my eyeliner, which had gotten kind of smudged. "You can do this," I told myself.

I tried really hard to believe it.

Don't miss any of the books in SWEET VALLEY JUNIOR HIGH,
an exciting series from Bantam Books!

Invisible Me

Written by
Jamie Suzanne

Created by
FRANCINE PASCAL

BANTAM BOOKS
NEW YORK·TORONTO·LONDON·SYDNEY·AUCKLAND

RL 4, 008-012

INVISIBLE ME
A Bantam Book / November 2000

Sweet Valley Junior High is a trademark of Francine Pascal.
Conceived by Francine Pascal.
Cover photography by Michael Segal.

Copyright © 2000 by Francine Pascal.
Cover art copyright © 2000 by 17th Street Productions,
an Alloy Online, Inc. company.

Produced by 17th Street Productions,
an Alloy Online, Inc. company.
33 West 17th Street
New York, NY 10011.

ISBN: 0-553-48725-6

Visit us on the Web! www.randomhouse.com/kids

Published simultaneously in the United States and Canada

Bantam Books is an imprint of Random House Children's Books, a
division of Random House, Inc. BANTAM BOOKS and the rooster
colophon are registered trademarks of Random House, Inc. Bantam Books,
1540 Broadway, New York, New York 10036.

PRINTED IN THE UNITED STATES OF AMERICA

OPM   0 9 8 7 6 5 4 3 2 1

To Laurie Wenk

Kristin

"Kristin," Bethel whispered in my ear.

"*Eeeee!*" I shrieked, and jumped back, crashing into the bank of lockers behind me. Bethel looked shocked, then doubled over in laughter.

"Thanks a lot," I grumbled. "Don't you know you shouldn't go around sneaking up on people like that?"

"Sorry, Kristin." I could tell that she was trying to stifle a laugh. Bethel McCoy is usually a very serious person, but right now her face kept smiling, then going straight, then smiling again—blinking on and off like a Christmas-tree light. That actually made me giggle a little bit. Then Bethel let out a hoot, and I totally cracked up.

"You-hoo-hoo looked li-hi-hi—" Bethel was laughing so hard, she could hardly get out the words. "Like I'd stuck an ice cube down your pants!" she finished in a rush.

I let out a snort, which made both of us laugh harder.

Laughing was such a relief—I'd been really

1

nervous all day. About what? Two words: class council. Ever since I became class president, I'd loved running the class-council meetings. But everything had changed when Ms. McGuire took over from Ms. Kern as our adviser.

Ms. Kern was my absolute favorite teacher. She always had a smile on her face and something nice to say. And she could turn even a not-so-great idea into something really excellent. For example, the eighth-grade class had recently thrown a carnival at school. Now, an idea like that *could* turn out extremely corny. But since Ms. Kern had helped with most of the planning, it had turned out great—and our class had taken in so much money at the carnival that we had a bunch left over. And even though Ms. Kern did a ton of the work for the carnival, she acted like all of the good ideas were mine and made me feel like the greatest president in the history of the eighth grade. But then Ms. Kern's mom got sick, and she had to move home to take care of her. Ms. McGuire became our new adviser, and everything changed. For the worse.

Don't get me wrong—Ms. McGuire isn't mean. Not exactly. It's more like she doesn't approve of what I'm doing. She wants me to be organized and on top of things, and I'm trying to be, but I still feel like I can never please her. Like, if I type up an agenda, she'll notice that I forgot to include a major item. Then she'll give me a lecture about professionalism—as if we couldn't just scribble whatever I forgot onto the margin! Hel-*lo*—this is student government, not Congress, for cripes' sake!

Anyway, the point is—today I was on a mission to show Ms. McGuire what an excellent class president I was. For the first week or so that Ms. McGuire was here, I'd started really doubting my abilities as president. But then I'd decided that I was really capable as long as I gave it my best shot. After all, hadn't more than half of my classmates checked the box next to the name Kristin Seltzer? If *they* had confidence in me, then she should too. I *really* wanted to impress Ms. McGuire. And as I stood in the hall laughing with Bethel McCoy, I started to think that it just might be possible.

Bethel wiped a laugh tear out of her eye. "Man! I've never seen anyone *jump* like that. Not even during a pole vault!" She's Madam Track and Field, by the way. "You must have been thinking pretty hard about something."

Was it that obvious? "What makes you say that?" I asked.

Bethel shrugged. "Oh, nothing. Just the fact

that I've been walking beside you since you left science class."

Science class? I thought. *That's all the way down this hall, around the corner, and halfway down the next!*

She and I fell into step as we headed toward the class-council meeting. "I can't believe I didn't even notice you," I said. "Sorry about that—I must have been zoning."

"No problem," Bethel replied. "I'm friends with Jessica Wakefield, remember? I'm used to dealing with cadets from the Space Academy." She grinned, her white teeth brilliant against her dark skin.

There was a while there—back when we were up against each other in the election for class president—that I wasn't sure if Bethel and I could ever be friends. But after the election she was totally cool with me, and she's always been completely supportive of me as president. Plus she seemed to know how to handle Ms. McGuire.

She turned her head to face me, swinging her hair over her shoulder. "Hey, new look!" I said. "I love your braids!"

Bethel smiled proudly. "Thanks. My mom did them for me last night."

"Oh, wow, your mom did those? They're so

fabulous!" I gushed. "*My* mom's idea of giving me a new look is telling me to go on a diet."

Bethel frowned. "You don't need to go on a diet. I've seen the way you eat—totally healthy."

I rolled my eyes. "Then why aren't I thinner?"

She shrugged. "Everyone has different body types," she said. "The key is just to be happy with who you are."

"I know you're right," I agreed. "But sometimes it's not so easy."

"So what were you so deep in thought about?" Bethel asked. "Gearing up for the meeting?"

Yes, I'm gearing up for the weekly Ms. McGuire organizational smack down! I wanted to say. But I held my tongue. For some reason, I didn't want Bethel to know that I was having problems with our new adviser. So instead I just said, "Yeah, I've got this great idea for what we can do with all the surplus money from the carnival." It wasn't exactly a lie. I *was* pretty excited about my idea—and I had taken a bunch of notes about it to show Ms. McGuire how systematic I was.

Bethel raised her eyebrows. "What's your idea?"

"Get psyched because the awesome idea is . . ." I swung my arms out wide. "Class trip!"

"Hmmm," Bethel said.

5

That wasn't exactly the response I'd been hoping for. "What's the matter?" I asked. "You don't think that's a good idea?"

"Where would we go?" Bethel sounded skeptical.

"Well, my two ideas so far are either the La Brea Tar Pits or the Huntington Museum of Art."

"You want to take our class to see some tar pits?" Bethel sounded like I had just suggested that we take a class trip to my *arm*pits. Jeez Louise, they're only one of the biggest tourist attractions in California! (The tar pits, not my armpits.)

"I went there with my mom and my cousins last summer. It's really cool!" I tried to sound excited. And I was. But it wasn't so easy to convey enthusiasm with Bethel staring at me like I was some kind of creature from outer space. "They have, like, the remains of mammoths there, all completely preserved. And then they also have giant replicas of saber-toothed tigers and all these other prehistoric animals. It's really awesome!"

"Mammoths? I *guess* that could be cool. . . ." Bethel was obviously making an effort to sound interested. It wasn't quite working, though.

"I brought some brochures for people to look at." I dug one out of my backpack and handed it to her. She flipped through it, then handed it back. *Okay, so maybe saber-toothed tigers aren't Bethel's thing,* I thought. But I wanted to convince her that it wasn't such a crazy idea after all. "You can look through the rest of the brochures at the meeting. I'm sure when people look at them and when I explain about the mammoths and stuff, nobody will be worried about visiting tar pits. I swear, it's a really great place."

And I was also sure that bringing brochures to the meeting would show Ms. McGuire that I had done some research.

"Hmmm." Bethel nodded. "Well, I definitely want to take a closer look at all of the info. What was that other place you mentioned? A museum?"

The way she said the word *museum* made it sound more like a form of torture than a fun excursion.

"Yeah, the Huntington Museum of Art," I answered enthusiastically. "It's this awesome art museum. They have tons of great sculptures and paintings and even art classes for kids."

Bethel cocked an eyebrow.

"Not that we're kids," I said quickly. "But maybe they could cook up a special class for us or something."

7

"I don't know." Bethel paused, like maybe she didn't want to say what she was going to. "It sounds more like an educational field trip than a class trip that's just for fun, you know?"

"Well, it would be educational," I admitted. "But it would be fun too. The tar pits and the museum are both *totally* fun!"

"I'm sure they are," Bethel admitted. "I'm just not so sure the class will go for it, that's all."

"I guess we'll just have to see at the meeting." I nearly laughed. "And I can guarantee you that Ms. McGuire will go for it. Teachers love all of that educational stuff."

"Yeah, I guess we'll see at the meeting," Bethel said.

Okay, so she didn't think my ideas were the greatest. But everyone else would. I was sure of it.

Blue

"Hey, baby bro, do you want me to drop you at the house on my way to work?" Leaf asked me as I helped him roll up the volleyball net after practice. "Or can you make it home on your own?"

"Work?" I nearly dropped the net. "You have to go to work tonight?" *Bummer,* I thought. Both my bother and I are pizza freaks, and postpractice pepperoni pies are our regular routine.

"Sorry, Blue." My brother shook his head. "The surfing game needs a lot of tweaking. We've got to demo it for the marketing guys tomorrow."

"Does that mean Gnarler is almost done?" I asked. I knew that Leaf had been putting in lots of hours designing his new video game, but I hadn't realized it was so far along.

"Yeah," Leaf said, his green eyes dancing.

"Well?" I prompted.

"Well, what?" Leaf was giving me his innocent look, but he was smiling.

I punched him lightly on the arm. "You know

what—how is it? Completely psychotic?"

Leaf shrugged. "I don't know about that," he said, "but Smitty said she thinks it's incredible."

"*Smitty* said that?" My jaw nearly dropped to the floor. Patricia Smits was the secretary—sorry, receptionist slash office manager—at my brother's video-game design place. Nobody knows how Smitty ended up working there, and it seems kind of strange that she does. Basically she thinks that video games are a bunch of nonsense, and she never gets excited about anything the company puts out. So if she thought the game was good . . .

"Gnarler must be way beyond rad!"

My brother laughed. "It's rad, all right. Maybe it'll be ready for you and your buds to give it a test run tomorrow."

"Awesome!" I held open the nylon bag so Leaf could stuff the rolled-up net into it. "I can't wait."

"Well, you're gonna have to wait—at least another day." Leaf waggled his eyebrows, then grabbed the bag and walked toward the equipment room. "So, you need a ride or not?" he called over his shoulder.

"Nah." I shrugged. "I invited Liz and Brian over for pizza, but maybe we'll go get some at Vito's instead."

"Cool." Leaf reached for his wallet. "Here's some money for pizza. I'll see you at home later—hopefully I won't be home *too* late. If it's going to be after eleven, I'll give you a call." Leaf handed me some cash. "And do me a favor— don't invite your friends over to the house. I know Brian and Elizabeth are superresponsible, but I don't like having a bunch of kids in the house when I'm not around to watch out for you guys, all right?"

"All right, dude." I nodded good-bye to my brother and turned around to look for Brian and Elizabeth.

All in all, living with my brother is pretty decent. I know he cares about me and is doing the best he can to bring me up right. Some people think I have the perfect life—I have this cool older brother who coaches the Sweet Valley Junior High volleyball team, loves to surf, and designs video games. Plus we live in this house on the beach, and there are no parents around to tell us not to eat too much ice cream. It's funny—you never think you'll miss something like your parents telling you you're not allowed to do stuff like that until it's taken away. . . .

"Blue!" Brian Rainey called from across the court, where he was standing with Elizabeth Wakefield. "Hurry up, man—it's pizza time!"

I grinned. "Hey!" I shouted. *Remember: left foot, then right foot,* I thought. *Don't trip.* The fact that the sunlight was streaming down and lighting up Elizabeth's golden hair like a halo made walking kind of difficult. This friend of Leaf's likes to talk about how everyone has an "aura." I don't know if I have one, but Elizabeth's can practically light up a room. She was wearing baggy shorts and a baby blue tank top, her blond hair pulled back in a ponytail. *How does she manage to look so fresh all the time?* I wondered. After all, we'd just been playing a hard game of volleyball. I sent a silent prayer to the gods of foul odor to keep me from smelling too rank.

"My brother has to work tonight," I announced when I reached Brian and Elizabeth by the exit door. "So—Vito's?"

"No Spiccoli pizza party today?" Elizabeth feigned horror. "Won't the world stop rotating on its axis?"

"Hey!" I pretended to be insulted. "I'm a *mobile* Spiccoli pizza party."

Elizabeth laughed, which practically made my whole week. "I'm up for Vito's," she said. "I just have to call my parents and make sure it's okay."

"I can go for a little while," Brian agreed. "But then I have to go home for dinner."

"Pizza, then dinner?" I teased. "How do you maintain that girlish figure?"

Elizabeth and Brian both laughed at that, and I felt like I'd just won some major award because I'd made Elizabeth laugh. *I'd like to thank all of those who made this moment possible,* I said in my head. *Especially Elizabeth Wakefield's blue-green eyes, for their inspiration . . .*

I was practically floating as I held open the door so my friends could walk out of the gym ahead of me.

It was another beautiful day in Sweet Valley, and I was happy to be sharing it with Brian and Elizabeth. Before I joined the volleyball team, I hardly had any friends at all at SVJH. I guess you could say I was kind of a loner. Not that I needed many friends. I mean, Leaf is really my best friend. But he's also my older brother and responsible for me and everything, so that makes it kind of different.

Of course, I did have a *few* friends before I met Brian and Elizabeth. Like, take Glenn, Leo, and Perry, for example. Some of my surfing compadres. They're ninth-graders—and they're outstanding surfers. That's awesome for me because even though Brian and Elizabeth are really cool, we aren't into the same kinds of things. Neither one of them likes to surf or anything, although

13

Elizabeth is kind of learning skateboard. Don't get me wrong, though. I still always have lots to talk about with them. Elizabeth is heavily into school, and she's, like, a very artistic writer and stuff. And Brian and I are starting a band together with Salvador del Valle and Damon Ross. It's called Big Noise.

"So what's your brother's latest game?" Brian asked as we walked toward Vito's.

"It's called Gnarler." I pantomimed a surfer stance. "It's a radical surfing game, totally realistic with three different beaches you can choose from: in California, Hawaii, and Australia."

"Wow!" Elizabeth said. "Have you played it yet?"

"Not yet. It isn't ready," I said, my thoughts suddenly drifting out to the ocean, where I couldn't help wishing I was right then. "But Leaf says that it might be by tomorrow. So maybe you guys can come over after practice and try it with me?"

Brian lifted his eyebrows. "Sounds great!"

I grinned—Brian is really into the fact that my brother's job is making video games and has even given Leaf some ideas for new games. I couldn't help glancing at Elizabeth. "You want to come over too?" I hoped I sounded cool, even though my brain was practically begging, *Please say yes, please say yes . . .*

14

"Oh, I can't tomorrow, sorry." Elizabeth looked kinda bummed.

"'How come?'" I asked her. There was no *Zone* meeting tomorrow, or I would have known about it. I'd joined the online 'zine Elizabeth and a couple of her friends had started a while ago, and I'd been going to meetings pretty regularly ever since.

"I promised Jess I'd go shopping with her." Elizabeth smiled. "She says she needs to *accessorize* her wardrobe."

"Next time, then." *I* was bummed Elizabeth would be spending the afternoon hanging out with her twin instead of me, but I tried to look on the bright side. *Hey, at least she sounded like she* wanted *to come.* "So it'll just be me and my man, Brian. It'll be a Rainey day."

"The forecast is Rainey, so watch out!" Brian agreed, grinning.

"And once I get those video controls," I added, "*you're* going to be all wet!" Brian laughed.

"Hey, speaking of all wet, check this out!" he said, pointing at a sign in Vito's window. "Sweet Valley Surf Contest," he read aloud. "All levels welcome. One-hundred-dollar cash prize for the winner."

"Whoa!" I turned to Brian. "Dude, we have to enter this!"

15

"*We?*" Brian threw back his head in a big, fat laugh. "No, no. I was thinking *you*, Blue."

"Well, have you ever surfed before?" I asked.

"Are you kidding? I am the *master*. I've surfed on WaveMasterFlash, SupaLongboard, and Shark Dodger III!" he joked.

"No, dude, seriously!" I looked him in the eye. "Have you ever surfed, like, in the waves?"

"No, man," Brian said.

"Well, I'll teach you. We can start tomorrow!"

"Are you serious?" Brian looked doubtful for a second. "Actually, that would be so cool. I mean, I've always kind of wanted to learn." He hesitated a moment, then added, "As long as you can loan me a board—I don't have one."

"You're going to teach Brian to surf?" Elizabeth's eyes got way big as she looked at me. "I'm so jealous!"

"I'd be happy to teach you too, Elizabeth," I volunteered.

"I'd love that!" she said.

My heart did a little flip-flop. It was the same kind of feeling you get when a huge wave is headed toward you, and you don't know whether you're about to surf the ride of your life . . . or get totally slammed by a wall of water.

"But listen, Blue, I don't think I'll be ready for a competition by *this* weekend," Brian pointed out.

Elizabeth looked dubious too. "Yeah, do you really think Brian's ready for a *competition?*"

"No worries, guys!" I spread my arms wide. "It's not like we're going to try to *win* the thing. I'm sure I wouldn't even *place* in an actual competition. But we can just do it for kicks. C'mon, it'll be fun."

"First things first," Brian answered. "Let's start with the lessons, and then I'll see if I feel up for the contest."

"Deal." I reached out to shake Brian's hand. "So tomorrow we'll get you out on the ocean, and then once your body is sufficiently thrashed, we can go back to my place for a little video surfing action."

"Oh, man!" Brian shook his head. "What have I gotten myself into?"

Bethel

"Okay, the next order of business is the annual canned-food drive," Kristin announced. I don't really know why she kept referring to "orders of business," but I guess she was trying to sound presidential. It came out sounding a little weird, though, like she thought we were on Capitol Hill. "Last year's drive was a resounding success, but I think we can do even better this year. Now, does anyone have any suggestions for how we can improve on last year's effort?"

I raised my hand, but Kristin didn't see me because she was staring at her neatly typed meeting agenda. She'd given us all a copy. Whoo-hoo.

"Well, if no one else has any input, let me share some of the ideas I jotted down before the meeting," Kristin announced. "First of all, I think we can collect more food for the needy if we make a contest out of it. For instance, instead of having one big barrel for cans by the main entrance to the school, why don't we have a barrel in each first-period classroom? That way whichever class gathers the most cans wins a prize."

I looked over at Ms. McGuire in time to see the corners of her mouth flicker down into a frown. She stood up from her chair at the side of the room. "Kristin, that *is* a very good idea. But before she left, Ms. Kern told me that there were some problems with that sort of system last year."

Kristin's cheeks flushed, and her mouth dropped open. "Really? Are you sure?"

"Positive," Ms. McGuire answered dryly. "For one thing, we don't want to reward people just because their parents can afford to donate more food than other parents."

"Oh." Kristin swallowed. She looked like she was at a loss for words.

"I have an idea," I announced, raising my hand.

Kristin shot me a grateful smile. "Bethel, you have the floor," she said in that weird official-sounding voice.

"Maybe we could have a small competition for which class brings in the most cans," I began, "and a larger contest for designing the best poster advertising the can drive."

"That's an excellent idea, Bethel," Ms. McGuire

said. She gave me a brisk nod. "It's a great way to build awareness for the can drive."

"That *is* a good idea," Kristin said slowly. "Would anyone like to make a motion? Bethel?"

"Yes. Thank you." I placed my palms on the desk in front of me. "I move that the eighth-grade class council sponsor a poster-design contest for the annual canned-food drive."

A bunch of hands went up around the room. Kristin looked at Jan Meier, one of my friends from the track team. "Jan?"

"I second that motion," Jan stated officially.

Kristin pounded on the desk with her gavel. "All in favor, raise your hands and say 'aye.'"

Even though everyone in the room raised their hands and said "aye," Kristin still asked, "All opposed?"

No one spoke.

"All right, then." Kristin banged her gavel once more. "The motion for the eighth-grade class council to sponsor a poster-design contest for the annual canned-food drive has passed unanimously."

Kristin sighed and looked around the room. "And now, for the next order of business, I would like a report from the eighth-grade dance committee."

I raised my hand.

Kristin looked confused. "Bethel, you aren't on the dance committee, are you?"

"Um, no. I'm not. But Ivy and Justin are both absent today, so I think we'll have to wait until next meeting to get a report."

"Good point." Kristin gave the table a quick smack with her gavel. "The next order of business is what to do with the surplus money that the council made from the carnival."

I stifled a groan. *Here we go,* I thought. I knew that Kristin was going to propose her idea of an educational class trip. And I was sure that no one on the class council would go for it. I mean, it was one thing to suggest a class trip to Disneyland. It's something else entirely to suggest a trip to the tar pits. But what could I do?

Kristin brought out a stack of brochures from her backpack. "Let me begin with *my* idea for spending the surplus money. I think we should use the money to pay for a big class trip."

"Kristin, may I interrupt?" Ms. McGuire asked. She didn't wait for an answer. "The school already has funding for field trips."

"But this wouldn't be a field trip—it would be a *fun* trip," Kristin cut in. She noticed Ms. McGuire frowning and backpedaled. "Not just fun, though. It would be educational too."

At the word *educational* groans erupted

throughout the room. Surprise, surprise.

Ms. McGuire sighed heavily. "What did you have in mind, Kristin?"

"Well, I had two ideas," Kristin started, shuffling the brochures on her desk. "The first is the La Brea Tar Pits."

"No way!" someone shouted from the back of the room. "My class took a trip there in the fourth grade."

"Well," Kristin said, her cheeks bright pink, "you must have gone to a very advanced school." Her voice got kind of shaky. "Or I was thinking we could go to the Huntington Museum."

"Oh, *great*. Another museum," came another voice from the middle of the room. Everyone in the class started grumbling and snickering about tar pits and museums. I felt bad for Kristin, but I had warned her about her ideas before the meeting.

"Silence!" Ms. McGuire stood up and faced the council to quiet everyone down since it was obvious that Kristin was losing control of the meeting. "Kristin, why don't we see if anyone else has ideas for using the surplus money?"

But Kristin wasn't ready to let go of her class-trip idea. "Well, we wouldn't *have* to go to a museum *or* the tar pits. We could go on a hiking trip instead."

"We could go on a trip to Universal Studios!" shouted Richard Griggs. "Then I could start my acting career!" He's under the mistaken impression that he's hilarious.

"If we want educational, maybe we should check out the Eiffel Tower in Paris," suggested Chelsea Sable.

The class council burst out laughing at that idea. Kristin looked like she was about to start crying. It's not like she's a good friend of mine, but still, I don't like to see anyone upset. I raised my hand. "Why don't we host an Olympics Day for the whole school?" I suggested quickly.

Ms. McGuire's eyebrows shot up. "An Olympics Day," she repeated. She rubbed her chin like she was seriously considering my suggestion.

"Yeah," I answered. "With different sporting events. Classes and individuals can compete against each other, and we can spend the money on ribbons and trophies for the winners."

A bunch of hands went up.

"Yeah, and we could make T-shirts for everyone," Jan shouted. "With different colors for the different classes."

"That's a great idea," Ms. McGuire gushed. "Does anyone else have anything to add?"

Kristin flashed Ms. McGuire a pleading look.

"I'm sorry, Kristin," Ms. McGuire said. "I didn't

mean to take over the meeting. Please continue."

Kristin looked out at all the raised hands. "Deena? Do you have a suggestion?"

Deena Spence nodded. "Yes. Why don't we have some silly competitions—like a water-balloon toss and a three-legged race—for people who aren't really that athletic?"

"Great idea!" I said. Kristin shot me a glare for speaking out of turn. Whatever. I understand that we need rules to make sure that the meeting stays orderly, but there is such a thing as taking it too far. Besides, why wasn't she grateful that I'd just saved her from the humiliation of her own lamebrain tar-pit idea?

"Kristin, would you like to call for a motion?" Ms. McGuire asked.

Kristin frowned. "You mean about Olympics Day?"

"Well, yes," Ms. McGuire answered matter-of-factly.

"Ms. McGuire," Kristin whined. "I still think we should consider my idea for a class trip." She held up her brochures. "I mean, I've gathered all this information on the tar pits and the museum, and nobody's even looked at it. Besides, we already put so much emphasis on sports at this school, and there's just so much more to life than track and field. . . ."

I decided to let that one slide, but Ms. McGuire cut her off. "Kristin, you obviously feel very strongly about your class-trip idea," she said.

"Yes, I do," Kristin huffed.

"Well, then," Ms. McGuire said calmly. "Why don't we give everyone a few days to think about their options? At the next meeting we can vote on your idea for a class trip and Bethel's idea for an Olympics Day. Does that work for you?"

Kristin looked like it didn't really work for her, but what could she say? "Yes, fine. Meeting adjourned." Kristin banged her gavel and flashed me a dirty look.

Top Ten Things I Will Say to Ms. McGuire When I Am Elected President of the United States

By Kristin Seltzer

10. No, you can't be secretary of state.
 9. Since I'm so *disorganized,* I'll just have to ask the chief justice to get back to you on that.
 8. I'm sorry, but you don't meet the new national teacher-niceness standards set forth by Congress.
 7. Talk to my secretary.
 6. No, you can't be head of the joint chiefs of staff!
 5. I'm sure your ideas about funding for extracurricular programs are very good, but I've got it covered. Thanks.
 4. I've declared the La Brea Tar Pits a national treasure.
 3. That's right, I'm taking the Senate on a "class trip"—to China.
 2. No, you can't be ambassador to France!
 1. Ms. McGuire, you stink!

Kristin

After the disaster at the council meeting the day before, I was actually happy to be in English class. I wasn't going to have to preside over anything, and I didn't have to worry about Ms. McGuire or Bethel McCoy shooting down any of my ideas.

English class was one place where most of my ideas were usually well received. Unlike Ms. McGuire, my English teacher, Mrs. Bertram, isn't an evil witch. In fact, she actually likes me and even thinks I'm smart. So I was looking forward to getting our latest assignments handed back. After my utter failure as president the day before, I really needed something to make me feel better. Something like a good grade on an English assignment.

We had been reading Homer's *The Odyssey*, and Ms. Bertram had asked us to write a four-page paper telling part of *The Odyssey* in our own words. I had decided to do something kind of different that I thought was more creative.

Instead of writing the same old boring *Odyssey* in my own words, I had turned Odysseus, the hero of the book, into a modern-day thirteen-year-old girl and made her adventures typical modern-life conflicts. I tried to pattern my writing style after Homer's, which I thought was pretty cool. Since Mrs. Bertram usually rewarded creativity, I thought she would get a kick out of my paper. For some reason my past few grades in her class hadn't been that great—probably because I hadn't been trying that hard. But I had put in so much work on the *Odyssey* paper that I was sure I'd get a good grade, and I'd be back on track in Mrs. Bertram's class.

Mrs. Bertram placed my paper facedown on my desk. I smiled up at her, and she hesitated, then looked away. *Uh-oh.* That was a bad sign.

I cringed as I peeled back the corner. *Oh no!* I turned the whole paper over to be sure that I was seeing correctly. A big, fat, red D was at the top, with a little note below that said, *Did not follow instructions. Please see me after class.*

I couldn't believe it. I had worked so hard. And I *did* follow the instructions. As far as I was concerned, I went *above and beyond* the instructions. I had shown how *The Odyssey* was meaningful to *me,* which is what I thought the assignment was all about.

I couldn't concentrate the entire period as Mrs. Bertram droned on and on about Homeric tradition. I kept thinking about our impending after-class chat. The last thing I wanted was to hear a stupid lecture about not following directions. She probably thought I didn't understand the assignment or something. But of course I understood the assignment perfectly. I just chose to interpret it my own way, which I thought Mrs. Bertram would appreciate. But she didn't, and now it was too late, so what use was there in talking about it?

When the bell rang, signaling the end of class, I gathered my things as quickly as possible and walked toward the door with my head down, hoping Mrs. Bertram would forget about wanting to talk to me. No such luck.

"Kristin, would you come here for a moment?" she said firmly before I could make it to the hallway.

I sighed. There was no getting out of it. I walked over to her desk.

"Kristin, I wanted to talk to you about your assignment," Mrs. Bertram began. "I appreciate what you were trying to do in your paper but—"

"But I didn't follow instructions," I finished for her.

"No, you did not." She sounded a little irritated.

"Now, would you like to explain why you didn't?"

"Not really," I answered. I really *didn't* feel like explaining myself. It never seemed to get me anywhere.

"So you have nothing to say in your defense, Kristin?" Mrs. Bertram tapped her foot.

"Nope," I answered. "I think it says it all at the top of my assignment. I didn't follow instructions, and you gave me a D, so I guess that's all there is to it." It wasn't like me to be rude to *anyone,* especially a teacher. But I just couldn't help being mad at how unfair Mrs. Bertram was being.

"And you have nothing else to add?" Mrs. Bertram tilted her head as she looked at me.

"I guess I'll just try harder next time," I replied with another sigh. "Now, if that's all, I should probably get to my next class."

"Fine," Mrs. Bertram said. She actually looked a little disappointed. "You may go, Kristin. And in the future please follow my instructions or see me in advance if you wish to interpret an assignment differently."

"Thanks. I will." I turned and walked out of the classroom. Could this day get any worse?

Brian

I was sitting outside with Blue Spiccoli during lunch when three surfer-type guys walked up. I had seen them around and thought they were ninth-graders, but I had never talked to them before. I guess they knew Blue, though.

"What's up, Spiccoli?" the tall, skinny guy with long, blond hair greeted him.

"How's it going, Glenn?" Blue smiled at the guy, then turned to the other two—one was short, and the other had tiny dreadlocks all over his head. "Hey, Leo; hey, Perry. What's goin' on, guys?"

I was always impressed with how cool Blue acted around everyone, even older guys like Glenn, Perry, and Leo. I guess hanging out with a hip older brother like Leaf must help. I have an older brother too, but hanging out with his dumb friends usually makes me feel like a dork.

"Nothing much," Leo answered. I think it was Leo. "We were just trying to decide if we should go to our next class or blow it off and go surfing.

The waves are supposed to be pretty gnarly today. Are you in?"

"Sorry, guys, I can't bail on class this afternoon." Blue gave them a half smile. I knew he was probably pretty tempted to go with them, but Blue had recently gotten into working hard in school. I knew that sweating over grades wasn't really Blue's style, but he seemed to like learning, and he was pretty smart. He didn't have to really work his brains out to pull decent grades the way I did. "Big, fat quiz during sixth period."

Glenn cocked an eyebrow. "Can't you just skip it?"

"I can," Blue admitted with a shrug, "but I won't. I'll be out there later—Brian and I are gonna take some runs after school."

The short one looked confused. "Who's Brian?" Perry asked.

Blue looked shocked and turned to me. "Dude, don't you know these guys?" I laughed and shook my head as Blue smacked himself on the forehead. "Sorry! That was so way rude! Brian, this is Glenn, Perry, and Leo, three of the raddest surfers at Sweet Valley Junior High."

"Three of the raddest surfers in *Sweet Valley*," Glenn corrected him.

Blue gave a little laugh and rolled his eyes.

"Three of the raddest surfers in the known universe—how's that, Glenn?"

Glenn thought for a moment. "Acceptable," he said.

"Hey, guys, how's it going?" I said, giving them my friendliest smile.

The three of them just nodded in my general direction without actually saying hi. Suddenly I felt like the freak of the week. I decided to just hang back and try to look mysterious for a while.

"Yo, Blue," said Perry, shaking out his tiny dreads. "Did you hear about the big surfing competition coming up?"

"Oh yeah!" I broke in. "That looks so totally rad"—the other guys were staring at me with superbored looks on their faces—"ical," I finished. "Radical." I cleared my throat. So much for mysterious.

"We totally heard about it," Blue said. He didn't seem to notice that I was nerding out. Or maybe he just didn't care. "That's why me and Brian are going out today—to start getting ready."

"Right on," Glenn answered without much enthusiasm.

"Leaf is supposed to be done with this killer new game today," Blue offered, changing the subject. "It's a surfing came called Gnarler. You guys should come over and try it out some time."

"Yeah?" Glenn suddenly sounded slightly more excited.

"Yeah, dude. Later this week, when Leaf's around, you can come over and take it for a test run." Blue smiled.

The three ninth-graders looked at each other and nodded. "Cool, yeah," Glenn said. "Definitely."

"Excellent." Blue high-fived his pals before they walked away.

"See ya," I added, but they didn't seem to hear me. "So those guys are friends of yours?" I asked when they were gone.

"Surf compadres," Blue corrected.

I wasn't sure how "surf compadres" were different from "friends," but I didn't ask. "That's cool," I answered, not quite knowing what else to say. I had been looking forward to my first surfing lesson with Blue. But that was when I thought it was going to be just me and him. Now that Perry, Glenn, and Leo were going to be there too, I was starting to feel a little nervous. I mean, what if I looked like a jerk out there? I pictured myself falling off my surfboard and having to get rescued by a lifeguard.

"So are you stoked?" Blue looked at me sideways and raised an eyebrow.

"Stoked?" I repeated.

"Yeah, for surfing this afternoon." Blue gave me a playful punch on the arm. "Are you ready to ride some killer waves or what?"

I took a deep breath. *Look on the bright side,* I told myself. Maybe I would get rescued by a cute lifeguard. "Yeah," I answered, trying to sound as stoked as possible. "Totally."

Bethel

It took Jessica Wakefield exactly fifteen seconds after the bell rang at the beginning of French to pass me a note. That had to be a record even for her. What did she do? Write them at home so she'd be ready for class? I unfolded the note as unobtrusively as possible.

How was the council meeting yesterday? it read.

Not bad, I wrote back. *I think we're going to spend the surplus money from the carnival on a schoolwide Olympics Day. My idea.*

I passed it back. When Jessica read what I had written, she let out a little squeak. Madame Vivienne, our French teacher, glared at her. "Would you like to answer that, Jessica?" she asked.

"Um," Jessica said with a grimace, "not . . . really?"

Madame Vivienne frowned and said, "We were discussing food. *Aimez-vous les pommes frites?*"

Jessica gave her a blank look. "*Un* Coca-Cola, *merci beaucoup?*" she guessed.

Madame Vivienne shook her head, then moved on to find another victim. At least Jessica's answer was somewhat food related; it seemed to satisfy Madame Vivienne. I guess after fifteen years of teaching, she knew not to ask for too much.

Jessica leaned over the note, scribbled something, then passed it back. *Track and field?* it said.

Yes, I wrote. *Plus soccer, basketball, volleyball, and so on. And some silly stuff too, like tug-of-war.*

Jessica read the note and nodded. Then she looked at me, her blue-green eyes sparkling. She wrote quickly, then passed me the paper.

So I'll finally have another chance to beat you in the eight hundred meters.

I nearly laughed out loud. *You'll have another chance,* I wrote, *to get beaten.*

I handed it back and grinned, remembering the first day I met Jessica. It was at tryouts for the cross-country team. I didn't think that she was the kind of girl who'd want to risk messing up her mascara by working up a sweat, so I didn't take her seriously. I challenged her to a race—big mistake. I nearly got dusted. *Nearly*.

"Get beaten?" Jessica whispered. She looked over at me, tilting her head and raising her eyebrows. "We'll just have to see about that." I knew that she half meant it—we're both pretty competitive—but she was smiling too.

"Yeah," I whispered back. "I guess we will."

"What are you two whispering about?" Madame Vivienne demanded. She marched over to Jessica and ripped the note out of her hands. "I suppose I should just read this to the entire class, hmmm?"

"Um—," I said.

Madame Vivienne held up her hand. "Silence!" Then she read aloud, "'How was the council meeting yesterday? Not bad. I think we're going to spend the surplus money from the carnival on a schoolwide Olympics Day. My idea.'"

A murmur of excitement ran through the class. Madame Vivienne looked up. I guess she realized that the note wasn't having the humiliating effect she'd hoped for, so instead of reading the rest, she just crumpled it up and threw it in the trash. Oh, well. I hoped the class council would vote in favor of Olympics Day at our next meeting because word travels fast at SVJH. I was sure that if we ended up going to the tar pits instead, there would be some seriously disappointed people in the eighth grade.

Then again, maybe the tar pits were an up-and-coming tragically hip scene (with all those dead, ancient animals and everything) that I was too uncool to know about. I had to admit it was possible.

I looked over at Jessica, who was trying her best to look interested in Madame Vivienne's lesson on how to order a dinner of fried eels in a restaurant. She turned to face me and crossed her eyes at the word *eels*. I stifled a laugh. That's one of the cool things about Jessica. She and I are rivals in track and field—but we're still good friends.

The bell rang, and Jessica and I gathered our things. "So, judging by the class's reaction to our note, it sounds like Olympics Day is going to be a big hit," she said as she crammed a purple pencil case into her book bag.

"Yeah, well, it's not totally confirmed yet," I admitted. "We still have to have a vote on all the ideas."

"Oh, really?" Jessica tossed her hair over her shoulder. "What are the other choices?"

"Well . . ." I hesitated. I was starting to feel bad about Kristin and her rejected idea. And I knew that Jessica would feel even worse—she and Kristin were tight. "Um, actually, Kristin thinks we should spend the money on a class trip." I tried to keep my voice neutral—would Jessica think the trip idea was a good one?

Maybe I was just biased against it.

Jessica looked interested. "To where?"

I hesitated. "Um—the La Brea Tar Pits?"

Her face fell. "Oh, man." Jessica crossed her eyes the way she had at the eel conversation, then heaved a heavy sigh. "Please tell me that the rest of the class council isn't into that idea."

"They aren't, really," I admitted.

Jessica shook her head. "What was Kristin thinking?" she demanded.

"That was the question on everyone's minds when she brought it up," I explained. All of a sudden I felt kind of bad for harshing on Kristin. "She had some other decent ideas," I said quickly. "She also suggested that we could go to the Huntington Museum of Art."

"Well, art is cool, I guess." Jessica swept a strand of golden blond hair out of her face. "And I suppose those tar pits might be *educational*—"

"Oh, spare me," said a voice behind us.

We turned around. Lacey Frells was walking behind us. I gave myself a silent kick in the rear for not being more careful about dissing Kristin's ideas—Kristin and Lacey are best friends. And Lacey sits right behind Jessica and me in French. *Duh.* I should have figured she would listen in on our conversation.

Jessica just ignored her. "So did Kristin have

any other ideas for the class trip?" she asked.

"Um . . ." I tried to remember. "Oh yeah, when no one really seemed interested in the tar pits or the museum, she suggested we take a hiking trip." Lacey let out a snort at that.

I sighed, then turned and gave her a cool stare. "Do you have something you would like to say to us, Lacey?" I asked in my best Madame Vivienne voice.

Lacey didn't crack a smile. "Yes, in fact, I do." She crossed her arms across her chest. "I think that a schoolwide Olympics Day is for dorks."

"Thanks for sharing," I said. Jessica looked at me and shrugged in a what-did-you-expect? gesture. I shrugged back. That kind of attitude from Lacey didn't really bug me—I was used to it. I turned my back on her, but Lacey grabbed my arm.

"I'm not finished," she said.

I cocked an eyebrow. "Please remove your hand from my bicep." I looked her in the eye, and Lacey dropped my arm like it had given her an electric shock. She's really not as tough as she wants everyone to think. "Lacey, if you'd rather spend a day with our class at an art museum or some tar pits, I'll be happy to mention that at the next class-council meeting."

Lacey gave her hair a toss and recovered. "Puh-leeze. I think all those stupid ideas are a waste of money." She straightened the straps of her book bag. "First of all, the tar pits are for tourists and three-year-olds. That's the kind of place that would be too lame even for my little sister. Second, the art museum is for old fogies. Like, the only people who go there are ones who have been pronounced clinically *dead*. I don't know what Kristin was thinking when she suggested those two things, but she clearly has no idea how old she is. Why don't we all just take a trip to the merry-go-round or to the old folks' home? Those places would probably be more appropriate." She gave a last snotty smile and turned to stalk off to her next class.

Unfortunately, when she turned, she came face-to-face with Kristin Seltzer.

Kristin

Why am I surprised? I asked myself.

For a long time I just stood there, staring at Lacey. I literally could not think of one single word to say. What on earth was she doing? She was dissing my ideas—to *Bethel?* Was I in some kind of parallel universe? The last time I checked, Lacey didn't even *like* Bethel, or Jessica, for that matter. I mean, *I* was better friends with them than she was, and here they were all gathered around, *mocking* me?

Actually, if I hadn't been so furious, I probably would have laughed at Lacey, who stood in front of me opening and closing her mouth like a fish. Then all of a sudden she straightened up and pulled herself together.

"Oh, hi, Kristin," Lacey said evenly.

Was she hoping that I hadn't heard her?

"Hi, Kristin," Bethel and Jessica chorused.

I gave them a little wave. Whatever. I knew Bethel didn't like my class-trip idea. That was her prerogative. And I hadn't heard Jessica say anything either way. But Lacey was supposed to be my best friend. As I saw it, it was pretty much her duty to defend my ideas, no matter how pathetic she thought they were.

I cleared my throat. "Lacey, can I talk to you for a minute?"

Lacey's smile faltered. "Sure, what's up?"

"See you later, guys!" I sang out to Bethel and Jessica. Then I steered Lacey down the hall.

"Quit rushing me," she hissed.

"No," I said. I led Lacey over to my locker, where I started getting out my books for the next class. I was still trying to think of what to say to her.

"Kristin, what's wrong?" Lacey asked in her most concerned voice.

"Lacey," I said, "your innocent act didn't work on me in the second grade, and it isn't going to work on me now." I slammed my locker shut. "I heard what you said about my ideas."

"So?" Oh, great. Now she was giving me the tough act. Like I didn't know them all by now. I sighed.

"So, I think it's pretty low of you to be ranking on me behind my back, especially to two people who aren't even your friends."

"Kristin, I didn't put *you* down," Lacey insisted. "I was talking about your stupid ideas, that's all."

I couldn't believe her! "*My* stupid ideas?" I demanded. "My *stupid* ideas?" Then, because I had no idea what else to say, I added, "*You're* stupid!"

Very mature, I know.

Lacey just rolled her eyes. "Come *on*, Kristin. What are you doing—campaigning for the school-spirit award?" She narrowed her eyes. "No offense, but those are the biggest kiss-butt ideas I've ever heard. Why didn't you suggest that we go on a class trip to pick apples for our favorite teachers?"

Kiss butt? Me? Who did Lacey think she was to talk to me like that? "Wha—You—Jus—Na—," I sputtered. I had plenty to say to Lacey about what a jerk she was being, but I couldn't get the words out fast enough. *"Aargh!"* I finally cried in frustration. I brushed past Lacey and stomped down the hall.

I was sick of it. Sick of Lacey. Sick of Bethel. Sick of class council—all of it. Sooner or later they'd all have to realize that the class-trip idea was a good one, and when they finally admitted it, I would give them all one huge *chunk* of my mind.

"Hey, Kristin!" Lacey called after me. "What did I say?"

Blue

"Uh, Blue?" Brian said. "Please don't take this the wrong way, but . . . I kind of feel like a loser."

I choked back a laugh. "Don't sweat it," I told him. "It's all part of the process." Poor guy. He was lying on top of Leaf's long board, pretending to paddle out. Unfortunately for him the board wasn't in the water—it was on the sand. Brian did look silly, but this was the best way to practice. It was how Leaf had taught me to surf eighty jillion years ago. "It's like *The Karate Kid*," I assured him. Brian and I had actually rented that movie recently. "You know, wax on, wax off." The main character in the movie is learning to do karate, and his teacher makes him do all these weird exercises—like waxing a car—before he actually teaches him to fight.

Brian sighed. "I guess this isn't as bad as having to paint the fence or something," he said. "I just hope nobody sees me like this."

Too late. I waved to Perry, Leo, and Glenn,

Blue

who were walking up the beach toward us. Oh, well. If anyone had to see Brian practicing on the sand, I was glad it was my surfer buds and not, like, his girlfriend, Kristin, or something. At least the surf dudes would know what we were doing.

When they caught sight of Brian, they stopped and elbowed each other. "Hey, Leo, check it out!" Perry shouted. "That turtle is laying its eggs in the sand!"

They laughed their heads off at that.

Brian looked humiliated. Actually, now that Perry mentioned it, he did look a bit like a mama turtle. I tried not to laugh.

The surf dudes walked over. "I'm teaching Brian the basics," I told them.

"The basics of what?" Leo asked. "Sand surfing?"

"Whoa, dude, watch out!" Glenn yelled. "A big, gnarly sand wave is coming your way!"

Brian jumped up and brushed the sand off his arms. "Hi, guys," he said. "Yeah, I think I'm about to surf a few of these big sand dunes, right, Blue?"

I smiled. That was just like Brian not to let some dumb comments get to him. He's a cool guy. I turned back to Perry. "Why don't you guys go on out in the water, and we'll join you in a minute?"

"Okay," Perry answered, clutching his short board under his arm. "I just hope we don't run over Mr. Long Board here."

"Long boards are the easiest thing to learn on," I answered.

I wasn't even sure the surf dudes had heard me. They were already running off into the waves.

As soon as they were gone, I continued the lesson. "Now, as long as you're comfortable with your balance and everything on your stomach, let's see if you can practice finding the sweet spot on the board with your feet."

"What's the sweet spot?" Brian asked.

"The sweet spot is like the perfect spot to stand when you're riding a wave," I explained. "It's where you're not too far back and you're not too far forward on the board. You're perfectly balanced, so the riding is, like, sweet."

"So right in the middle of the board?" Brian asked.

"Not exactly," I answered. "Every surfer and every surfboard has a slightly different sweet spot. You'll have to find what feels right to you."

"So are we going to go practice that in the water now?" Brian asked hopefully.

"No way! Are you kidding?" I had to laugh at Brian's cluelessness. I tried to remember the first time Leaf took me surfing, but it wasn't easy. I felt like I had been surfing my entire life. "Standing up on your board when it's in the water is really hard. I guess it comes naturally to some people. But most people don't even get to stand up on their first day out. Sometimes it takes a few days before a person can get up. I'll be really impressed if you can even ride a few waves on your knees today."

"So, more sand surfing." Brian groaned. I could tell that the other guys ranking on him had made him sort of self-conscious.

I nodded. "Sorry, Brian," I said. "Let's just see if you can find the sweet spot here on the beach—or at least practice finding it because you can never really be sure until you're out on a wave. And then we'll go out in the water."

At the word *water* Brian seemed to perk up. "As you wish, master," he said, giving me a goofy Karate Kid bow.

He stood on the long board and tried finding the sweet spot, but like I said, it's hard to tell if you've got it until you're out on a wave. Then I had him practice getting up on the board from his knees to his feet.

"Now, you have to stand up in one fluid motion," I explained to Brian. "That's the most important thing about surfing. You have to be fluid. Like the water."

"Fluid, like the water," Brian repeated.

I demonstrated again, and he imitated me. "Great!" I told him. I had a good feeling—Brian was a good imitator and a very patient person, and those are the two most important things when you're learning to surf. Patience, especially. I picked up my board and gestured out toward the ocean. "Are you ready?"

"Ready as I'll ever be," Brian answered.

"All right, let's go." I slapped Brian on the back. We both fastened the leashes of the boards around our ankles, and we walked out to sea.

We waded in until the water was over our knees, and then we both laid our boards on top of the water. I got on my belly and started paddling out. Brian tried to lie down on his board, but it capsized, and he tumbled into the shallow water.

"Whoa!" Brian yelled as he lost his balance.

"See?" I grinned. "It's a lot easier when you're on the beach, right?"

"I guess so," Brian agreed as he scrambled onto his board again. This time he managed to balance himself, and we both started paddling out with our arms.

We finally made it out to where the waves were breaking. Perry, Glenn, and Leo were already there, waiting for some tasty waves to ride.

We lined up near them, but not too close. I didn't want Brian to get in their way and mess up their rides.

"Now, you've got to wait for the apex of the wave before you can drop in," I explained to Brian.

"Wait a second." Brian was short of breath and sounded slightly panicked. "What does 'drop in' mean again?"

"That's when you stand up on your board and ride the wave," I told him. "Just remember, you need to get up in one fluid motion."

"Right, one fluid motion," Brian repeated. "So how do I know when the apex is coming?"

"The apex is the top of the wave at the moment it's breaking," I explained. "Don't worry— you'll know it when you see it."

"But what if I don't?" Brian asked, sounding confused.

"Trust me, you will," I promised him. "But if you're not in position to catch the apex, then you have to let the wave pass over you."

"So how do I do that?"

"Well, there are two ways," I told him. "You can either duck dive or turn turtle."

"And in English, those things translate to . . . ," Brian prompted.

"Okay, English." I sighed. Teaching someone

to surf was a lot harder than I thought it would be. I looked over at Leo, who had just caught a wave and was riding it in. A big part of me wanted to be showing off with the other surf dudes, not here going over the basics with Brian. "Duck diving is when you point your board toward the wave and just shoot through it nose first," I told him. "It's like you're ducking under it and coming out the other side."

"I get it," Brian said. He was frowning, like he was concentrating superhard on remembering what I was saying. "So what's turtling?"

"Turtling is when you spin upside down in the water so that your board is above you and the wave passes over your board," I explained. "And then after the wave is by you, you turn over again and get back on top of your board."

Brian grimaced. "I'm not so sure about that move," he confessed.

"Just try duck diving for now," I suggested. "It's easier."

Brian practiced duck diving and wiped out a few times before he even attempted to ride a wave. Each time he came to the surface, he splashed around a minute, struggling to find his board again. Luckily it was leashed to his ankle. I stayed there with him, but I was getting antsy. I wanted to start surfing.

Whoa, I thought, noticing a big, tasty wave, *think of the devil.* "All right, Brian, there's a big, juicy curl coming our way," I alerted him. "I'm gonna ride this one. And I suggest you do the same. Just remember: one fluid motion."

The wave broke perfectly, and I caught the apex just as it reached me. I dropped in and felt the familiar heart drop as I started riding it toward the shore. I glanced over my shoulder to look back at Brian. He almost managed to stand up, but he was too far forward on his board. He nose-dived. The back of the board popped up behind him, sending Brian face first into the water.

After my ride I got back on my stomach and started paddling toward the break. "Hey, Blue!" Perry yelled. "Did you just see your buddy eat that saltwater sandwich? Bwah-ha-ha!"

The other guys were laughing too. But I wasn't. I paddled out to where Brian was just getting back on his board. "Dude, your first major wipeout!" I said to him. "Are you all right?"

Brian grinned. "Yeah, I think so," he answered. "Actually, that was kind of fun!"

"Well, I'm glad you think so"—I gave him a high five—"because there's plenty more where that came from."

My New Surfing Vocabulary
By Brian Rainey

Bowl: A shallow place in front of the wave. (Watch out—this can make a wave break hard!)

Log: A long board.

Green face: The part of a wave that is not breaking; the smooth face of a wave that you are riding—or *trying* to ride.

Tube: When you are surfing totally inside a curl. (This has not happened to me and probably never will.)

Takeoff: When you grab the sides of your board and stand up. This is generally the beginning of a ride. In my case it is the beginning of a fall.

Short board: A board five feet long or less. What the cool kids use.

Brian

I made it through my first day of surfing alive. *At least I think I'm alive,* I thought as I rubbed my sore left shoulder. I'd wiped out about a hundred times, but the only thing that was seriously sore was my ego. Oh yeah, that and my arms, shoulders, legs, feet, and the back of my head, where the board smacked me during my final run.

But I still felt pretty good. The reason the board hit me was because I finally stood up. I was up for only about one second, and it was the only time I made it up all day. But according to Blue, that was a success.

Now I was just happy to sit on the beach and watch Blue and the other guys. It was amazing— somehow they made it look so easy. All four of them were joking and laughing out in the ocean, finding just the right waves, dropping in and riding them effortlessly. I tried to see what they were doing so I could learn from them, but it was so hard to figure out. Everything just looked natural.

Brian

They paddled out, found the perfect wave, waited for the exact second to get up, rose to their feet, dropped in, and rode the wave as far as it would take them. Simple.

So why couldn't I do it?

I had to keep reminding myself that it was my first day out. After all, Blue, Leo, Perry, and Glenn had all been surfing for years. For them it *was* simple. And if I stuck to it, I knew that I'd get better too.

Especially since Blue was such a good teacher. Even when the other guys were laughing their heads off at my lack of surfing talent (and who could blame them? I bet I looked hilarious), Blue had kept cool. He never laughed when I wiped out, and he kept giving me pointers on my technique. And when I finally did stand up, he got really excited. Like he had made a breakthrough too.

And now we had one more thing in common besides school, volleyball, and our band, Big Noise. That was totally cool with me. Recently I'd been kind of worried that Kristin and I were spending a little too much time together. Don't get me wrong—I love hanging with her; she's the greatest. But I felt like I wanted some more time to do stuff with my guy friends. Different stuff. Like surfing, for example.

At last the guys decided to call it a day and started heading in toward the beach. When they got off their boards and started walking across the sand, I could tell that they were just as tired as I was. But they weren't too tired to give me a hard time about my lack of surfing skills.

Perry spoke first. "Hey, Brian, was this your first time surfing or something?"

I nodded. "The very first."

"Yeah, we could tell." Perry smirked.

"So, how's that ocean taste, Brian?" Leo chuckled.

I'm not very good with clever comebacks, so I tried to think of what my older brother, Billy, would say in this situation. "I forget," I said. "Why don't you go chug some and tell me?"

"Ooooooh!" Perry and Glenn laughed and pointed at Leo, who turned bright red.

"Shut up, dudes," Leo told them.

I looked over at Blue to see his reaction. He half smiled and then looked away. Suddenly I felt kind of bad. I hoped I hadn't made Blue mad by razzing his friend. I was just kidding, you know?

"So what's the plan, Blue?" Perry asked. "Are we gonna go to your house and try out that new surfing game or what?"

Blue pursed his lips and tilted his head. "Oh, well, Leaf left a message on our machine and said it's not quite done yet. He's probably going to be at the studio until pretty late finishing it up."

Even though I had been looking forward to trying the new game, I was slightly relieved to hear that it wasn't ready. I'd had enough surfing for the day, whether it was real or video.

"Aw, bummer, man." Glenn slicked his wet hair back with his hand. "I was all jazzed to check it out."

"Whatever, Blue," Perry said. "You still have plenty of other games at your house, right?"

Blue hesitated. "Um, yeah, I guess. . . ."

"So let's just cruise over to your place and play something else." Perry made a gesture to his crew.

Blue looked down at the sand. "Uh, I don't know. My brother doesn't really like me to have people over when he's not around. Maybe we should just wait for some other day, like when the surfing game is done."

"Aw, come on, Blue," Perry said. "It's cool. Leaf knows us."

"Yeah," Leo agreed. "I'm sure he wouldn't mind us hanging around for a couple of hours." Obviously these guys didn't want to take no for an answer.

"I don't know. . . ." Blue looked over at me as if I could somehow bail him out of the situation. I just shrugged. What could I say?

"So just call him up and ask if it's cool," Glenn suggested.

"Yeah, there you go, Blue." Leo picked up his board like he was ready to go. "Just call him up when we get to your house and ask him if it's cool. What's he gonna say? 'No'?"

"Oh, I don't think so, guys." Blue was starting to sound a little flustered. "Leaf doesn't like me to call him at work unless it's an emergency."

"Aw, dude, you are so soft." Perry kicked some sand at Blue, then looked at his other friends. "What's the matter? You gotta go home and do some homework? First your stupid quiz is more important than catching some waves with us, and now you don't want to hang and play some video games? Whatever, Blue, we can take a hint."

"Come on, Perry, you know it's not like that." Blue jumped to his feet. "I totally dig hanging with you guys. And you're right—I'm sure it'll be cool with Leaf if you guys come over. Like you said, he knows you. I'm sure he won't mind."

"Cool." Perry reached out and mussed up Blue's scraggly blond hair. "I knew you'd come around. Let's go."

I just sat there in silence, debating whether or not to join them. I wasn't really crazy about Blue's friends. Then again, Blue was a really cool guy. So maybe his friends weren't as bad as I thought. And maybe they'd give me some surfing pointers if I hung out and got to know them better . . .

Blue turned back when he noticed I wasn't with him. "What's up, Brian? Is everything cool? You're not sore or anything, are you?"

"Of *course* I'm sore, man. Are you kidding?" I looked up at Blue and tried to smile, tried to look happy to be hanging with his older surfer buddies even if I wasn't. "But everything's cool, man. Totally."

Kristin

"What's wrong, honey? You've hardly even touched your chicken." My mom reached across the dinner table and gently stroked my shoulder.

"Nothing, Mom." I shrugged, not wanting to talk about the disaster that my life had become. "I'm just not very hungry."

"Kristin, this is very low fat," my mom said, which made me want to lunge across the table and strangle her. My mother is very tall and slim and doesn't understand how her very own daughter could be average height and slightly pudgy. And she *really* doesn't understand how her daughter could be slightly pudgy and not care about losing weight. I, on the other hand, can't understand how she has room in her brain to count fat grams. I can barely remember my multiplication tables. I simply don't have the mental energy or space for remembering the number of calories contained in five ounces of chicken.

"Mom, I don't care about the fat in this chicken, okay? I'm not eating because I've got some stuff on my mind."

Mom looked hurt, which made me feel kind of bad. I sighed. "Sorry, Mom," I mumbled, and picked up a forkful of broiled potato.

"What's wrong, Kristin? Talk to me." Mom put down her fork and leaned toward me. "Forget about dinner if you don't feel like eating. Let's just talk."

I shook my head. "I'm just having some problems with the class council, that's all. See, we've got some money left over from the carnival," I explained, "and I had this idea to use the money to pay for a class trip to the La Brea Tar Pits or the Huntington Museum or hiking or something."

"Sounds great." Mom smiled at me. "So what's the problem?"

"The problem is, nobody else thinks it's a good idea."

"Well, I find *that* hard to believe." My mom frowned. "Are you saying that nobody in the eighth grade wants to go on a trip?"

"Well, no one on the eighth-grade *class council* wants to go on a trip," I admitted. "The rest of the class doesn't know about my suggestions."

"Hmmm." Mom took a delicate sip from her

water glass. "Well, did anyone else have any better ideas about what to do with the surplus money?"

I rolled my eyes. "Bethel McCoy came up with this stupid idea of having a schoolwide Olympics Day."

"That doesn't sound very educational," my mom said.

"Tell me about it!" I agreed. "But Ms. McGuire was totally behind it. So now everyone thinks it's a brilliant idea, and they think *my* ideas are stupid. And when we vote on the ideas at the next meeting, I just know I'm going to lose."

"Oh, sweetheart," my mom said soothingly. "I'm sorry to hear that."

"Well, it wouldn't have been so bad if it didn't feel like Bethel and Ms. McGuire were totally ganging up on me," I explained. "First Ms. McGuire was on my case the entire meeting, and then every time Bethel had an idea, it was like she fell in love with it. And the same went for everyone else in the room too. Maybe I *shouldn't* be president after all."

"Oh, Kristin, don't say that." My mom got up out of her chair and came over to give me a hug, which was just what I needed. I was already starting to feel better. "You've been an excellent president. You've worked so hard, and you've got so many good ideas, and all of your class-mates really like you."

"Yeah," I huffed. "All of my classmates *used* to like me." I didn't want to go into the whole thing about Lacey.

"Don't be silly," she scolded me. "Now, didn't you say that the council still has to vote on which idea you're going to spend the money on?"

"Yes," I replied.

"Well, then, your idea still might win," my mom reasoned. "In fact, I'm sure it will as long as you put your energy into convincing the council members that it's a better idea."

I thought about it. Mom did have a point. I had kind of given up on my idea the minute everyone didn't come out and say it was the greatest thing they'd ever heard. Maybe I just needed to point out that not everyone in our grade was into athletic stuff. Like me, for exam-ple. Then again, with Bethel and Ms. McGuire behind Olympics Day, I wasn't really sure that my idea had a chance. . . .

Still, I wasn't ready to give up. Not yet. And that went for my English grade too. Why hadn't I tried to convince Mrs. Bertram that my *Odyssey* paper deserved better than a D?

Since when had I become such a quitter?

I would convince my English teacher to give

me a better grade. And maybe the class council thought Olympics Day was a great idea, but I didn't, and I was the one who the eighth grade had elected class president.

So if the council didn't agree with me, they could . . . they could . . . well, go jump in a lake for all I cared.

An Olympic-sized lake.

Blue

"Leo!" I shouted. "Watch out!"

"Huh?" He whirled around and stepped right into the piece of pizza that Perry had set on the floor. I sighed. I'd seen this coming from a mile away. Leo's foot and the pizza slid right off the paper plate, grinding tomato sauce, green peppers, and extra cheese into the carpet. He held up his foot and looked at the disgusting mess dangling from it. "Oh, man!" he said. "Nasty!"

Brian jumped out of his chair. "I'll get a paper towel," he said, sprinting into the kitchen.

"You loser," Perry said. "That was the last piece of pizza! And stand aside—I can't see the TV!" Perry leaned around Leo to see what his commando guy was doing. I could see that he was mostly getting gunned down by Glenn's commando guy. The surf dudes had been playing Commando Joe for two hours straight. They took the game very seriously. A little too seriously, if you ask me.

Leo stepped out of Perry's way, tracking

73

tomato sauce across the floor. "Stop moving," I told him. Leo looked at me, and I made a stop motion with my hands. "Stay very, very still."

Leo just nodded.

I shook my head. Couldn't they even say something like, *We're sorry, Blue, that we're so lame. We're sorry that the fact that we don't know how to eat like normal people means your older brother will never let you invite anyone over to your house ever again.*

Oh, well. Seriously, what did I expect? This was my own stupid fault for not being able to say, "No, guys, you can't come over today. We'll hang another time."

I knew Leaf wouldn't be too psyched about me bringing Brian and a bunch of boneheads over to the house when he's not around—especially without asking ahead of time. He probably wouldn't have minded so much if it were just Brian. But these other guys were a different story. Especially when they started leaving bright red footprints all over the house.

Brian burst into the living room with a roll of paper towels. I went to the closet and dug out the carpet cleaner. Believe it or not, this wasn't the first time that someone had spilled something all over the carpet. Once Elizabeth—who is totally not the irresponsible type—spilled a soda all over the floor right before my brother and I were expecting a social worker's visit. It was really important to me to have everything look perfect for the visit, so I kind of flipped out. Ever since that day I've insisted that we be ready with heavy-duty carpet cleaner just in case.

Brian helped Leo clean most of the mess off his foot. Then Leo hopped to the bathroom to wash his leg in the bathtub. I squirted the cleaner onto the carpet and started scrubbing. Brian helped out. Perry and Glenn clicked their controls and shouted as their video commandos kicked each other in the head.

Brian smiled at me. He'd been kind of quiet ever since we'd gotten back from the beach. I figured he was probably just beat from his first day of surfing. He'd done really well, though. Most people can't stand up at all on their first day. Brian was a total natural.

"Wipeout!" Perry cried as the head of Glenn's commando rolled across the video screen. "Dude, you're toast!"

Glenn slammed down his controls. "This game bites," he said.

Perry turned to Brian. "Are you ready to get your butt whipped?" he asked.

Brian gave him a half smile and said, "No thanks. I'm kinda tired."

Perry snorted. "Whatsa matter? You afraid you'll get beat . . . the same way you did out in those waves today?"

Brian just stood there a minute, like he wasn't sure how to respond. Now, I happen to have personal experience with Brian's video-game skills. And let me tell you, they are *dangerous*. I personally thought that it was pretty likely that Brian didn't want to humiliate Perry and was just trying to spare his ego by not playing Commando Joe. But of course, Brian would never *say* that. So maybe he was just tired and didn't feel like playing. I guess I'll never know because Brian never responded to Perry. He just turned to me and said, "Blue, where should I throw these dirty paper towels?"

"In the kitchen, under the sink," I told him.

"Give me yours too," he said. I put my dirty towels on top of his pile, and he headed to the kitchen.

As soon as Brian left, Perry turned to me and said, "Don't take this the wrong way, Blue, but your friend is *beat*."

I stared at him. "Um, how am I supposed to take that the *right* way, Perry?"

Leo walked in from the bathroom just in time to hear that exchange, both of his feet much cleaner than they'd been even before the pizza incident. "Yeah, Blue," he said. "Brian couldn't surf his way out of a glass of water, man."

I was getting pretty fed up. "You guys should chill on Brian, all right? I bet none of you guys could get up for, like, the first four times you went out."

"Dude," Glenn chimed in, "you are *not* serious about him entering the surfing contest, are you?"

"Yeah, why not?" I shot back.

"Because he can't surf. Like we keep telling you," Perry answered. "If you bring him to the contest, you'll be the laughingstock of the entire SV surf scene. C'mon, even *you* were laughing when he went over the falls." Perry crouched into a surfer's stance. Then his face shifted into a look of horror as his arms flailed wildly and he tumbled to the floor.

I laughed. I had to admit, it was a pretty good imitation. Going over the falls is when you try to drop in too late, and you end up getting munched by the waves and churned around under the water like you're stuck inside a washing machine. It happens to everyone at one point or another, but Brian's face had been totally priceless.

"All right, all right," I said. "It's not like I think Brian is going to collect any trophies at the contest. Except maybe in the category of Most

Saltwater Consumed—" We all cracked up again.

"Hey, Blue," Brian said from behind me. Uh-oh. I turned to face him, cringing. I hoped he hadn't heard that. . . .

"I think I'd better get going," he said.

"Um, are you sure?" I said lamely.

"Yeah, it's getting kind of late, and I have to be home in time for dinner or else my mom freaks out." Before I could stop him, Brian quickly gathered his stuff and headed for the door. "Thanks for the lesson, Blue," he called on the way out. "Later, dudes."

"Later," Perry, Glenn, and Leo chorused.

"Much later, man," Glenn added, and the others cracked up.

I didn't feel like laughing. I felt more like kicking myself. But instead I just decided to kick the other guys out. "Listen, my brother's gonna be home pretty soon," I told them. "I gotta clean up and stuff."

"I thought he was working late," Perry protested. "We were just gearing up for another round of Commando Joe."

"Yeah, well, I've got some stuff to do, okay?" This was actually true. I had a ton of English homework, and I was sort of hoping I'd have a chance to call Elizabeth and get her advice on it before it got too late. I picked up the empty pizza box. "Besides, don't you guys have homes of your own?"

"Yeah," Leo admitted. "But they don't have pizza and cool video games."

"Shut up, butt head," Perry heckled Leo as he threw his sweatshirt at him. "Let's leave little boy Blue here so he can do his chores."

They piled out of the house without even offering to help. Or saying good-bye, for that matter. I shut the door and turned to face the living room, which was piled high with dirty cups and napkins. Considering that I'd never called my brother to tell him that the guys were coming over to play video games, I had a lot of work to do to get things cleaned up before he got home. I sighed. It didn't look like I'd have time to call Elizabeth and get her help with the homework after all. If I even had time to do it, period.

"Thanks, guys," I said to the empty room. "Thanks a lot."

Bethel

"Please come to order," Kristin shouted as she banged her gavel on the desk. "Our only order of business today is to decide which activity we will sponsor with the surplus money from the carnival. The two suggestions were a class trip or a schoolwide Olympics Day. Ms. McGuire has informed me that the winning idea will be announced at tomorrow's school assembly."

"That's correct, Kristin," Ms. McGuire agreed. "*You* will make the announcement at the school-wide assembly."

I yawned. I'd had to get up an extra half hour early for this "special meeting" Kristin had called. I looked around the room. Everyone else looked just as sleepy as I was. And just as grouchy. The only one who seemed wide awake was Kristin.

"Okay," she said. "Before we take a vote, I think we should review the pros and cons of each idea. Bethel, would you like to remind everyone why they should vote in favor of Olympics Day?"

What? Was I supposed to have prepared a list of reasons why we should sponsor an Olympics Day? Nobody had warned me about this. Now I was going to look like a jerk in front of the entire class council.

I thought about refusing to speak, but everyone in the room was looking at me expectantly. I sighed and stood up. "I think an Olympics Day would be fun," I said. "People at SVJH like sports, and they like to compete. This would be a good way to get whole classes to work together as teams and to value different classmates' skills. But most of all, I think everyone will just have a good time. Plus it won't be that expensive." I sat back down. I knew my speech wasn't terrific, but it would have to do. I was too tired to think of anything else.

"Thank you, Bethel," Kristin said in her official voice. "Now I will give the reasons in favor of a class trip." She whipped out a manila folder and took out a stack of papers. The members of the class council groaned. This had *long, boring speech* written all over it.

Kristin ignored them. "Reason number one: educational value," she read from her paper. Next to me, Deena Spence was creating an elaborate doodle involving the gods on Mount Olympus. Only they all had name tags with the first names of members of our own student council on them. I stifled a giggle. It looked like I got to be Athena. ". . . and the core principle of advancing our minds means that we should undertake . . . ," Kristin droned on.

I heard a soft snore coming from Richard Griggs, in front of me. I gave his desk a quick kick. He started, then shook his head, like he was trying to clear it.

"Point number four: school spirit," Kristin went on. Would this never end? How many points did she have? *Less than ten; tell me it's less than ten,* I thought.

". . . building a greater sense of community among our peers." She took a deep breath. "And finally," Kristin said. At that, the room burst into spontaneous applause. Kristin looked up from her paper, blinking. She smiled a moment, as if she thought everyone was cheering for her brilliant idea. Then I guess the truth hit her, and a deep pink blush spread across her face. She looked like she might cry. My heart went out to her. But what could I do?

Ms. McGuire stepped in. "Thank you, Kristin, for those insights," she said. "Now, if everyone has made up his or her mind, I think we should call for a vote."

Nice save, Ms. McGuire, I thought.

"Right, thank you," Kristin said, managing to regain her composure. "All those in favor of spending the surplus money on a class trip, please raise their hands."

No hands went up.

Kristin looked around the room, desperately searching for at least one person to vote for her idea. I considered raising my hand for her sake but decided that would look like the pity vote it was.

Kristin sighed heavily and spoke in a tired and defeated voice. "All those in favor of the Olympics Day, please raise your hand."

Every hand in the room went up, and a few people even cheered. I know that I should have been thrilled, but when I looked at Kristin's face, I just felt really sorry for her even though she *had* brought it on herself.

I was about to say something, but finally Ms. McGuire's voice piped in. "Now, Kristin, since we still have more than ten minutes before the first bell, I suggest we use this time to brainstorm ideas for the Olympics Day. That way you can give the school a few details about the event when you make your announcement tomorrow." Kristin nodded, and Ms. McGuire added, "Would you like to begin a discussion?"

Kristin sucked in her breath before she spoke. "Yes. Okay. Now, who would like to begin?"

A bunch of hands went up, and Kristin started calling on people. She actually did a pretty good job of hiding her feelings or at least not freaking out. But I could tell it wasn't easy.

I wished that she could just lighten up. If she got into the idea of the Olympics Day, then she could really do a lot to make it a successful event. I mean, Kristin was the driving force behind the carnival, and that was an awesome day. If we could just work together on this, I knew it would be a success. And we might even have fun working together.

"Bethel." I heard Kristin's voice as if from a distance. "Bethel!"

I snapped to attention. "Yes?"

"Since Olympics Day was your idea, is there anything you would like to add before the first bell rings?" Kristin asked. I just sat there a moment, completely stunned.

For some reason, I couldn't come up with a single decent idea for Olympics Day.

Kristin

I don't usually pat myself on the back, but I have to say this about the class-council vote: I remained calm.

I did not go over and kick Ms. McGuire in the shin, even though that was what I wanted to do. I couldn't believe she didn't even let me finish my presentation! She just jumped right in there, calling for a vote before I'd even made my last point. If that didn't prove that she was trying to force the class council to hold Olympics Day, then I didn't know what did.

This whole thing was all about Ms. McGuire and what *she* wanted. And clearly she wanted whatever her favorite, Bethel, wanted. It was ridiculous.

And I just didn't think it was fair that the class council was going to force the entire eighth grade to have an Olympics Day when I was so sure that everyone would much rather take a class trip. I mean, what about the kids who weren't into athletics? What about the kids who came to school to *learn?* It was so unfair—not just to me, but to everyone.

So, anyway, I kept my cool. I helped brainstorm ideas for Olympics Day. And as soon as the first bell rang, I left that room and walked into the hallway, ready to burst into tears. I kept my head down as I rushed through the crowded hall toward the bathroom. Everyone was just arriving at school, and the hallways were jammed.

In my watery-eyed haze I saw Jessica and Elizabeth walking toward me. "Hey, Kristin, are you all right?" one of the twins asked. I'm not sure which one it was. I don't usually have much trouble telling them apart, but then again, I'm not usually avoiding eye contact because I'm about to start sobbing.

I faked a smile in their direction and headed into the girls' room. I took a few deep breaths. Looking in the mirror, I tried to give myself a pep talk.

"Get ahold of yourself, Kristin," I said softly. "Don't let them get to you. You're class president, and you're going to show that class council that you're a good leader and that your ideas are good ones." I nodded firmly, then tried to even out my eyeliner, which had gotten kind of smudged. "You can do this," I told myself.

I tried really hard to believe it.

Granny Knows How to Cha-Cha

By Big Noise
Lyrics by Salvador del Valle

She may only be five-foot-one,
But she knows how to have some fun.
And she may be over sixty-three,
But she still seems to outdance me.

You may think she's an old lady,
But I've got news for you—
Granny knows how to cha-cha.
Granny knows how to cha-cha.
You may think that you're a hotshot,
But Granny knows how to cha-cha.
Don't step on her toes
'Cause Granny knows
How to cha-cha!

Even though her hair is a little blue,
On the dance floor she knows what to do.
All the other dancers give her looks,
But that's because her dancing really cooks.

You may think she's an old Doña,
But I've got news for you—
Granny knows how to cha-cha.
Granny knows how to cha-cha.
She'll drop you like a hot pot,

'Cause Granny knows how to cha-cha.
Don't step on her shoes
'Cause Granny proves
She can cha-cha!

Blue

"So when is the next Big Noise rehearsal?" Salvador del Valle asked me as he, Elizabeth, and I stood by his locker, killing time before class. "I've been writing lots of songs."

Big Noise is the band we recently started with Brian and Damon Ross. I play drums, and Salvador's the singer. Brian plays sax, and Damon is on guitar. As Leaf likes to say, Big Noise is a band that "really captures a sense of man's struggle with musical instruments."

"You've written some songs?" I stared at Salvador. "Wow, I wish I could write one."

"It's easy," Salvador assured me.

"I guess," I told him. "But sometimes it's just hard to get inspired." I couldn't help looking over at Elizabeth. I'd been trying to write a song about her—even though I didn't want her to *know* it was about her. But it was really hard to say how I was feeling. Elizabeth smiled at me and nodded sympathetically.

"Writing can be really difficult," she said.

"Sometimes it's hard to find a subject."

"Oh, I don't know." Salvador was looking past me down the hall, where a rowdy group of guys was making a lot of noise. "I tend to find inspiration everywhere," he said absently. He seemed distracted, so I followed his gaze . . .

And saw Perry, Leo, and Glenn. "Hey, Blue!" Perry called, and the surf dudes jogged over.

"What's up, man?" Leo said to me.

"Hi, guys. These are my friends Salvador and Elizabeth." Salvador gave them a little wave. They totally ignored him and sort of gave Elizabeth the eyeball (like I said, she's really pretty), all without actually saying anything. I guess it's against their code or something. I'm the only eighth-grader I had ever seen them talking to.

Perry smirked. "So where's your girlfriend?"

I noticed Elizabeth jerk her head in my direction at the word *girlfriend*. Oh, man. I didn't want her to get the wrong idea. I wanted to shout something like, *What do you mean—I don't have a girlfriend—I'm totally and completely available, and as a matter of fact I would like to have a girlfriend but don't,* but I couldn't think of a way to make it sound natural. I looked over at Salvador to bail me out, but he was just standing there, looking kind of shocked.

Lucky for me, Leo joined the jerk club and cleared up everything. "Yeah, where's your girlfriend?" he repeated. "What's his name? Brian?"

"Man, when are you guys going to let up?" I pleaded.

"As soon as you decide not to enter the contest with him," Perry answered.

My surfer buddies were really starting to get on my nerves, but I had to admit: They had a point. Maybe Brian really didn't have any business entering the contest. Still, I wasn't going to dis Brian just because they were giving him a hard time. Especially not in front of Salvador and Elizabeth, who were both Brian's good friends—just like I was supposed to be.

"So what?" I finally said. "Brian's my friend. If he wants to enter the contest, then I'm not going to tell him not to."

"Whatever, dude." Perry shrugged and shook his head. "But if I were you, I'd save yourself the embarrassment and ditch that kid before the contest."

"Well, you're not me," I answered. "So I guess it's up to Brian whether he enters the contest or not. Either way, I'm going to totally back him up."

As I might have expected, Glenn and Leo started mocking me. "Oh, you're such a supportive friend, Blue," Glenn said sarcastically.

"Let's all gather round and give each other a big hug!"

"I think you've been watching way too much *Oprah*," Leo added.

"Dude, no more Lifetime channel for you," Perry said, and he and Leo high-fived each other.

Salvador sort of jerked forward, and I could tell he was about to jump in with some scathing remark, but Elizabeth put her hand on his arm, and he backed off. I couldn't think of anything to say, so I just said, "Whatever."

The three ninth-graders walked away, shaking their heads.

"Um, are those guys . . . friends . . . of yours?" Salvador asked after the three of them were out of earshot.

I didn't really want to say yes, but I couldn't say no, so I settled on, "I guess."

Elizabeth and Salvador were giving each other a look that said, *Should we tell Blue that his friends are jerks?*

"Yeah, they like to kid around," I said quickly. "It's not like I hang out with them that much. Mostly just down at the beach. You know, they're just surfing buds."

Luckily the bell rang and we all had to go to separate classes. I didn't feel like talking anymore.

I knew that Perry, Glenn, and Leo weren't the most sensitive guys around. But I had to admit that they had a point about Brian. He *had* just learned to surf, and he wasn't really very good yet. What if he embarrassed himself at the competition and it was all my fault for encouraging him to enter? If he gave up surfing because of that, it would be majorly bad surf karma for me. And I didn't want that to happen.

But most of all, I didn't want Brian to hate me forever.

We're Jerks

By Big Noise
Lyrics by Salvador del Valle

We strut down the hall,
We talk really loud,
We shove you aside,
We're in the cool crowd.

We're jerks! We'll make fun of your friends.
We're jerks! We'll take your lunch money.
We're jerks! We love to offend.
We're jerks! We think we're real funny.

We're older than you,
And we're half as smart.
We won't laugh at your jokes,
So don't even start!

We're jerks! You will be so amazed.
We're jerks! We act like we're tough.
We're jerks! It's the way we were raised.
We're jerks! And we'll never grow up.

Brian

"Mmm-hmm," I said, "mmm-hmm. Well, why don't you—mmm-hmm. Mmm. Yeah, but—ah. Aha. Well, did you think—mmm. Mmm-hmm." It was after dinner, and I was on the phone with Kristin. I was trying really hard to be sympathetic and cheer her up and everything, but it was hard when I couldn't get a word in edgewise.

Kristin had just spent the past half hour telling me about the D she got on her English paper and the fact that Ms. McGuire hated her guts. Unfortunately the whole conversation was pretty vague, and I wasn't sure what the real problem was exactly.

She finally paused to take a breath, and I jumped in. "Can I say something? Kristin, you're just having a bad week—that's all. Why don't we just look at everything that's gone wrong, one by one, and see if we can find a way to make it all right again?"

She sighed. "Okay." I heard a thunking noise in the background.

"Did you just nail a two pointer?" I asked her.

"Yes," she admitted.

"Then I know it's serious," I said in a grave voice. Kristin has this habit of taking a rolled-up pair of socks out of her dresser and tossing it across her room into the wastepaper basket, which usually then slams against the wall. She only does it when she's concentrating—and only when she's on the phone. The first time she and I had a serious phone conversation, I thought she was knocking her head against the wall or something. The thing about it is, she always hits the shot. If she and I were to play sock ball, I know she'd take me down in two seconds flat.

Kristin just laughed. "Okay. Let me start by telling you everything that's been going on with the class council. Because I think that's my biggest problem right now."

"Okay," I said. I wanted more than anything to help Kristin destress, but I had problems of my own, so I was a little distracted. I kept thinking about Blue's surfer buddies. I wasn't sure if I could hang out with those guys again, but I definitely liked hanging with Blue.

Maybe I should just stick to Big Noise and forget about surfing. That way I could avoid seeing Perry, Glenn, and Leo. But that would mean bagging on the surfing contest, and I knew Blue was totally into the idea. And I thought it sounded kind of fun too, even though I was guaranteed to look like a certified idiot. Maybe it would turn out to be as much of a good time as Blue said it would be.

But enough of my problems. Kristin needed me, and I wanted to come through for her. Unfortunately, just as I was beginning to refocus on the conversation, I heard a beep.

"Hey, Kristin, can you hold on for a second?" I asked. "That's my other line."

"Okay," she said, sighing.

I clicked over. "Hello?"

"Yes, may I speak with Mr. Rainey, please?" a grown-up voice said. It was for my dad. I thought it might be someone selling something, so I asked who it was.

"Lance Peterson," said the voice. "Is this Billy?"

"It's Brian," I said. Billy is my older brother. I've got a brother and three sisters, so my parents' friends always get us mixed up.

"Oh, Brian! I think I met you last year during a dinner party at your house."

"Yes, hello," I answered, even though I had no idea who I was talking to.

"Listen, Brian," Mr. Peterson said politely. "I hate to bother him at home, but I just need to ask your father if he can sit in on a meeting with me tomorrow. Can you put him on, please?"

"Sure," I answered, as cheerfully as possible. "Just a second."

I knew that Kristin wouldn't be too happy holding on for this long. But then again, if my dad found out he missed a business call, he'd be even more upset.

I clicked back over to Kristin. I felt really awful that I hadn't been even a little bit helpful about her problem. "Kristin?" I asked. "Sorry that took so long, but it's for my dad." I tried to remember what the guy had even said. "He has to sit in on a meeting tomorrow or something. I'll call you back as soon as they're done talking about work, I promise."

Kristin paused. "Don't worry about it, Brian. Um, I can just talk to you in school tomorrow."

"Listen, Kristin, I really want to help you with your problem. I'm sorry about this call—"

"Really, it's okay. I understand. And actually, I think you have *helped* me. Totally. You're the greatest, Brian."

I stared at the receiver. I'd helped? I smiled. *Great!* I didn't really do anything, but if Kristin felt better, that was enough for me.

That's the cool thing about girls.

They're so weird.

Lacey Frells Spends a Wild Night at Home

7:15 P.M. Lacey's stepmother, Victoria, tells Lacey to get her feet off the couch. Lacey rolls her eyes and turns off the TV, then walks up to her room.

7:17 P.M. Lacey dials the first three digits of Kristin's phone number to complain about Victoria, then remembers that she and Kristin are in a fight and hangs up.

7:18–8:10 P.M. Lacey flips through *Fourteen* magazine, silently mocking the fashions.

8:12 P.M. Lacey's three-year-old half sister, Penelope, wanders into Lacey's room, asking to play a game. Lacey suggests hide-and-seek. When Penelope runs off to find a hiding space, Lacey locks her door and returns to her perch on her bed to flip through *Fourteen*.

8:47 P.M. Lacey's stepmother bangs on her door, demanding to know why Penelope was crying at the back of the walk-in closet. Lacey insists that she has no idea why and suggests that perhaps Penelope needs child counseling.

8:48–9:05 P.M. Stepmother lecture #1,407.

9:07 P.M. Once her stepmother finally leaves, Lacey picks up the phone. She dials the first three digits of Kristin's phone number again before remembering that they aren't speaking. Furious, she slams down the receiver, causing the plastic to crack. Lacey gives up, gets in bed, and decides to stay there forever.

Kristin

Brian Rainey is the best boyfriend in *the entire world. And he's a total genius, but he doesn't even know it.*

I looked down at the stack of flyers in my hand. I hadn't had time to print out that many—just about thirty—but I figured that if I put one in every third locker or so, people would pass the word around. I'd worked really hard on making the flyers eye-catching so that people would pay attention to them.

Preassembly Demonstration!
Your eighth-grade class council wants to
force you to have an Olympics Day!
If you don't like that idea, come to the
anti-Olympics-Day sit-in!
Meet in front of the auditorium
five minutes before assembly.

I smiled. *This should get the response I'm looking for,* I thought. If the class council thought they could force Olympics Day down the throat of the Sweet Valley Junior High eighth grade, they had better think again. As the class president, it was my duty to make sure that the entire class supported how we chose to spend our funds. Still, I didn't want anyone (like Ms. McGuire, for example) to get the wrong idea and think that I was trying to undermine the class council. That's why my name wasn't on the flyer and why I hadn't mentioned the class-trip idea on it. I would just happen to show up at this sit-in organized by some unknown students, and I would just happen to mention my class-trip idea. When everyone agreed that a class trip was a terrific idea, they'd head to the assembly and demand that we decide between Olympics Day or class trip by a full-class direct vote.

It was a brilliant idea. And it was all thanks to Brian, who told me that his father had to "sit in" on a meeting.

I had actually started to giggle at the thought when I spotted something that wiped the smile right off my face. And her name was Ms. McGuire.

"Oh, Kristin, there you are," Ms. McGuire said breathlessly as she rushed up to me. I shoved the flyers into my locker and slammed it shut. Luckily Ms. McGuire didn't seem to notice anything. "I was hoping I could catch you before class," she went on.

"Well, you caught me," I answered in my most cheerful voice. "I'm all ready to make the big Olympics Day announcement right after lunch." I felt a little guilty for lying, but then, this was *Ms. McGuire*. She'd been making my life torture since I'd met her.

"Kristin, I think we need to talk," she said firmly. She placed a hand on my shoulder and looked directly into my eyes. "Can we step into my office for a second?" I nodded and followed her into her office at the end of the hall.

"The truth is," Ms. McGuire said, closing the door behind me. "I'm very concerned about you."

I frowned. What was she getting at? "What are you concerned about?" I asked.

"Well, you seemed very upset at yesterday's meeting," she said. "And I've got some serious concerns about your role as class president."

My heart started beating faster, and I could feel myself beginning to sweat. "Ms. McGuire, what do you mean?"

Ms. McGuire stared directly into my eyes. "What I mean, Kristin, is I want to make sure that you really think being class president is the right thing for you now."

"Of course it's the right thing for me," I snapped back defensively. "I was elected, wasn't I? Didn't the eighth grade choose me?"

"Listen, Kristin," she said firmly. "It just seems that you're under a tremendous amount of pressure right now." She paused for a moment. "And if you think it's too much for you to handle, then I don't want you to pressure yourself into thinking you have to do it all. There are other people who are very capable and willing to work hard."

I couldn't believe it—she wanted me to step down! And of course I knew who she meant when she said that "other people" were capable and willing to work hard. She meant Bethel, of course! Her little pet.

I tried to keep my voice as even as possible as I answered. "Ms. McGuire, I have to admit that I've been under some pressure with my classes as well as the council. But I don't want to stop being president."

Ms. McGuire looked at me and gave a slow nod. "Okay, Kristin, I'm going to trust you on this one." She smoothed back a strand of hair that had escaped from the tight bun she always wore. "I just wanted to make sure that *you* felt up to the job. But if it ever gets to be too much for you, I want you to come to me so we can talk about it, understood?"

"Yes, of course I will." I managed a smile and added, "And thank you for being so understanding. I won't disappoint you."

"Great." A brief, businesslike smile flitted across Ms. McGuire's face. "I'll see you at the assembly, then," she said, and strode off down the hall.

I opened my locker and looked at the stack of flyers waiting for me.

"You bet you will," I said softly.

Brian

"Hey, Brian, have you seen Kristin today?" Lacey Frells asked me as I walked into the cafeteria.

"No, and I was just about to ask you that same question," I said, feeling suddenly worried. Where was she? Maybe our phone conversation hadn't gone as well as Kristin said it had. I knew I should have called her back to check in. "I was hoping to catch her before school and smooth things out. But she wasn't at her locker."

"I know. I couldn't find her this morning either." Lacey frowned. "We had a little fight the other day, and I was hoping I'd have a chance to apologize."

Apologize? Lacey? Now I was really worried. I hoped Kristin wasn't seriously upset over something. "I hope she's okay."

"Yeah, me too," Lacey said. She looked more concerned than I had ever seen her look about anything.

It was strange. The two people I wanted to

talk to were Kristin and Blue, and I couldn't find either of them anywhere. "By the way, have you seen Blue Spiccoli around today?"

"Blue Spiccoli? Is he that weird surfer guy?" Lacey crinkled her nose like she smelled something rancid. "I don't think I've seen him, but I doubt I'd remember it if I had."

"Oh, well, thanks," I said politely.

That was Lacey for you. She never had anything nice to say about anyone except for maybe Kristin. "So, if you see Kristin, tell her I'm looking for her, okay, Brian?" Lacey asked.

"All right," I answered. "You do the same, okay?"

"Yeah. Later." Lacey walked off toward the salad bar, and I followed my nose to the hot food.

I stepped into the hot-lunch line, psyched that they were serving spaghetti. For some reason, SVJH has the best spaghetti and meatballs. Most of the other food is pretty disgusting, but the spaghetti is all right. I knew Blue liked the school spaghetti as much as I did, and I half expected to see him in line. I looked for his head of tousled blond hair in the crowd waiting for hot lunches, but he wasn't there.

But that didn't mean I was alone. Nope. Lucky me—Leo, Perry, and Glenn stepped into line right behind me. I'd never noticed them before Blue introduced us, but now I seemed to run into them everywhere. I tried to think of a way to get out of line—should I slap my forehead, like I'd just forgotten something really important, and then just jog off? Or should I say something out loud like, "I've only got one minute to get to my Spanish tutorial—I guess I'd better skip lunch!" In the end, I decided to just suck it up and stay in line. After all, I wasn't crazy about these guys, but they were Blue's friends. Besides, hadn't I thought they might be able to give me some pointers on surfing?

"Hey, Perry, what's up?" I gave the guys a half wave. "Hey, Leo; hey, Glenn; how's it going?"

"Oh, hey, *Brian*." Leo said my name like it was a joke in and of itself, which irritated me. "How ya feeling today, buddy? Are you still sore from *surfing?*"

The other two guys cracked up.

"I'm doing fine," I told them. "How are you guys? Did you get the pizza stains out of your sock, Leo?"

Leo looked defensive. "I threw those socks out, dude," he said.

I shrugged. "Whatever."

"Man, whatever," Perry said. "He's just jealous

because he and his little friend don't know the way of the wave."

Me and my friend? Was he talking about *Blue?*

"Seriously," Leo agreed. "At least Brian here has an excuse. Blue's skills are *totally* over-hyped."

"Man, that kid is not nearly as cool as he thinks he is," Glenn put in.

"What?" I demanded. "Aren't you guys supposed to be his *friends?*" I shook my head. Who did these guys think they were? "Blue could go totally around bragging about how what a good surfer he is and what a cool guy he is, but he never would. Instead he just hangs around with you jerks. And personally, I have no idea why."

Had I actually believed I could ever put up with hanging out with these losers? No thanks. I never wanted to see them again—on a surfboard or off one. They were perfectly happy to be hanging out at Blue's and using his stuff, but now they were ranking on him in the middle of the cafeteria for everyone to hear. It was totally uncool.

"Listen up." Leo poked me on the chest. "You don't know Blue half as well as we do, okay? And I can tell you right now that little guy thinks his skills are twice as rad as they are. And he thinks that his brother is cool just because he has a few tattoos."

"Totally." Perry nodded.

"Then why do you guys hang out with him?" I asked.

All three of them burst out laughing. "We hang out with him because he's got a rad beach house and a killer video-game collection, doofus." Perry pointed at his head. "Think about it."

"Now, I'm not telling you this to make you feel bad," Leo went on. "I'm just telling you to save you some pain, just in case you're expecting your buddy to actually do well in the competition. You and Blue should just stay out of our way in the water. We'll let Blue know when we're ready to hang out at the house."

"Oh, I don't feel bad," I assured Leo, "because I know something about Blue that you *don't* know."

Perry folded his arms across his chest. "And what's that, genius?"

I smiled. "I know that he's standing right behind you."

Kristin

I stood off to the side of the auditorium doors. This was going to be my shining moment, and I couldn't wait. My fellow classmates and I were going to reclaim our right to decide whether or not to have Olympics Day. The power of the people! It would be like the French Revolution, only nobody would have to get beheaded.

The first bell for the assembly rang, and students started streaming past me. I tried to look inconspicuous as I checked out their faces. Who would join my cause?

"Olympics Day sounds so great!" Mary Stillwater said to Marlee Randall as they passed me into the auditorium.

Hmmm. That didn't sound so promising. Oh, well, a few of the students were bound to think Olympics Day was a good idea—especially jocks like Mary and Marlee. But all I needed was 51 percent of the eighth grade to think Olympics Day was stupid, and I'd still win.

"Hi, Kristin!" Lindsey Warner walked up to me with a huge smile on her face.

"Hi!" I said. Then I lowered my voice. "Are you here for the sit-in?"

Lindsey looked shocked. "No way! I want you to know that I got one of those flyers in my locker this morning, but I told all of my friends not to go. We totally support Olympics Day, Kristin. It sounds like another one of your great ideas." She gave me a little wave and trotted into the auditorium.

Another one of my great ideas? But it wasn't my idea! That's when I realized that nobody in the eighth grade could possibly have known that—unless he or she was on the class council.

As my classmates flowed past, I looked for someone, anyone, to join me. *Please don't let me be the only one who thinks Olympics Day is stupid,* I begged silently. *Please—*

That's when Ronald Rheece jogged up to me. Ronald is slightly dorky, but at that moment he could have been a mass murderer and I would have been happy to see him. "Are you here for the protest?" he whispered urgently.

"Yes!" I said. "I'm so glad that you see what a silly idea Olympics Day is, Ronald." *Naturally he sees how silly it is,* I told myself. *Ronald is the smartest kid in the whole school, if not the whole state!*

"Of course I do." Ronald nodded seriously. "And I have a great idea for how to spend the surplus carnival money."

"Class trip?" I asked hopefully.

"Mathletics competition," he replied.

I stood there, confused. "Wh-What?" I stammered.

"*Math*letics competition," he repeated. "I think there's too much focus on sports at this school. I'd like to see a new academic competition instead—like in math and science. After all, isn't the school supposed to be focused on education?"

Oh. My.

Did Ronald Rheece seriously think that he could force the entire student body to spend their extra money on some dumb math contest just because that was what *he* wanted? Obviously nobody would want to do that. . . .

With a jolt, I realized something very important. That's what *I* was doing.

I'm being really childish by trying to short-circuit Olympics Day, I thought. Clearly everyone—except myself and Ronald—thought the idea was awesome. Why was I trying to stand in the way?

But suddenly I knew the answer to that question too. I was standing in the way because the idea wasn't mine. I'd set out to show Ms.

McGuire how smart and organized I could be, and now I'd taken it too far by turning into a total control freak! I'd tried to force my class-trip concept down everyone's throats, when the truth was they just weren't interested. I was so ashamed.

And now I couldn't go in there and face the council and the rest of the eighth-grade class— not after how I'd acted. Not when I suddenly felt like I didn't even deserve to be up at that podium.

"I'll see you later, Ronald," I said, turning to run down the hall.

"Wait! Where are you going?" he called after me. "Don't you want to hear about my ideas for Mathletics Day?"

I didn't even bother to say no.

Bethel

"Pssst!" Jessica buzzed in my ear from the seat behind me. "Where's Kristin?" she whispered urgently. "Isn't the assembly about to start?"

"Yes," I answered in a hushed voice. "And I don't know where she is."

The principal, Mr. Todd, stepped up to the microphone to start the assembly. I looked around the auditorium for a sign of Kristin, but she was nowhere to be seen.

Mr. Todd introduced Ms. McGuire, who was then supposed to give a short speech about the carnival surplus before introducing Kristin. I wondered if Ms. McGuire knew that Kristin wasn't even here. She was supposed to be sitting right next to me, along with the other class officers in the front row.

"Good morning, students and faculty of Sweet Valley Junior High," Ms. McGuire began. "First let me tell you all how much I've enjoyed my first weeks working as the student-government

adviser. The group of students I've had the plea-
sure of working with has been outstanding." She
paused to smile as our classmates cheered. I had
to laugh. The eighth grade is known for cheering
at anything.

"Last month's school carnival, organized by
the eighth-grade class, was one of the most successful student-produced events in the history of
the school. And much of the credit for its success belongs to our eighth-grade class president,
Kristin Seltzer. Kristin has been an invaluable
asset to her class and to student government at
Sweet Valley Junior High."

I looked toward the door to see if Kristin had
come inside the auditorium yet, but there was
still no sign of her. How could she not show up
for an assembly where she was supposed to be
making an announcement? It wasn't like her at
all—she was usually so responsible.

Ms. McGuire continued. "So it is now with
great honor that I introduce her: Your eighth-
grade class president, Kristin Seltzer." On cue,
the eighth grade erupted into applause.

When Kristin didn't appear, Ms. McGuire
looked uncertainly into the crowd. "Kristin?" she
asked. "Would you come up here, please?"

An awkward silence fell over the auditorium.
If Kristin didn't show up soon, someone was

going to have to take her place. And I guessed I was the one who would have to do it. I anxiously looked around the auditorium one last time, but she still wasn't in the room. After another ten seconds of confused silence, which felt like ten years, I got up and approached the stage. Whatever. Impromptu speaking was becoming my specialty.

Ms. McGuire flashed me a look of surprise and relief as I took the podium.

"Ahem. My name is Bethel McCoy, and I'm eighth-grade vice president. Unfortunately our class president, Kristin Seltzer, could not attend the assembly this afternoon. So I will now make the announcement concerning how our class will spend the surplus money from the carnival."

I looked out into the crowd, again searching for Kristin. But my eyes kept drifting back to Ms. McGuire, who was standing on the side of the auditorium, wearing a concerned frown.

Blue

"I'm telling you, surfing is not an Olympic event," Brian insisted.

"That's what I'm saying," I agreed. "That's why we need info on surf competitions to get them to include surfing in *our* Olympics Day."

After the school assembly Brian and I had walked to the library. I figured it was important to make sure that my sport was represented, and I planned to give the evidence to Brian's girlfriend, Kristin. She was heavily into student government, and I figured that she could get the class council to include surfing in Olympics Day.

"But how will we get people from the school to the beach?" Brian asked.

"Details, details," I said. "We'll run a shuttle bus or something. We'll convince the class to have a beach barbecue at the end of the day, and we'll hold the surf contest then."

Brian just shook his head. "Okay, Blue. Here's another article on the surfing world championships."

"Awesome!" I said. I grinned at Brian. I knew

that he thought my idea about including a surfing contest in Olympics Day was pretty lame.
But I also knew that he would never say so because he was my friend.

After he'd stood up for me to Perry, Leo, and
Glenn, he and I had just left those guys standing
in the cafeteria with their mouths hanging open.
Needless to say, the surf dudes won't be coming
to any Spiccoli pizza parties in the near future.

"Listen, Blue, about surfing . . . ," Brian said
slowly. "I wanted to talk to you about the competition this weekend."

"Oh yeah?" I wondered if he still wanted to
enter. "So what's up? Are you still stoked?"

"Not exactly." Brian looked at me, then
looked away. "I'm not sure if I want to do it
after all."

"Why not?" I asked, already kind of knowing
the answer.

"I just don't have the skills, Blue," Brian answered apologetically. "And I don't want to make
you look bad in front of your friends."

I had to laugh at that. "What friends?" I
asked. "If you're talking about Perry and those
guys, you don't have to worry about it. Clearly
they aren't my friends, dude. And nobody else is
going to care." Then I remembered how I'd
made fun of Brian's lack of skills. And when I

thought about how he'd stood up for me today, I felt pretty low. "Listen, Brian. I don't know if you heard me talking about your wipeout, but I wanted you to know that I feel really bad about that. . . ."

Brian waved his hand like he was swatting away a fly. "Don't worry about it. I mean, it was funny when I took that dive. And I know you would have laughed if it had happened to anyone else too—and even if it had happened to you. You didn't mean it as a dis."

"Yeah, I didn't," I agreed. "But I'm sorry if that's how it sounded when you walked in. Man, I still wish I'd done a better job of defending you—the way you did when Leo was talking about how great I think I am."

"No big deal," Brian said.

I nodded. "Okay. Well, thanks."

We sat there in silence for a minute. Then I said, "And about the surf contest. You should do it only if you want to. Personally, dude, I think it'll be fun. And I'm definitely not expecting to win or anything. I'm just doing it for kicks, and I thought it would be cool to have a good friend there with me. But if you don't want to enter, that's totally cool with me."

"So you won't be embarrassed if I totally stink?" Brian asked.

"No way!" I had to laugh. "And you definitely don't stink. You're a natural, dude. I was serious when I said that it was totally rad that you managed to stand up on your first day. Not even I could do that—my first day, I mean. And if you keep surfing, you'll probably be better than me someday."

"Someday in the very distant future." Brian clicked on the screen, searching for more surfing info. "It was pretty fun, though, getting out in the water."

"That's what it's all about," I said. "Having fun. So I think we should just do it. That is, if you really want to."

Brian flashed a wide smile. "I'm in. Let's go for it."

Kristin

When I got home from my long day of roaming around by myself, my mom was waiting at the kitchen table. She didn't look too happy.

"Kristin, where have you been?" Suddenly I felt horrible for not calling to tell her where I was. "I've been worried sick about you!"

I didn't want to lie, but I also didn't want to tell my mom that I had cut the second half of school. So I sort of told her part of the story. "I'm sorry, Mom. I should have called you—I went to the mall after school." It wasn't exactly a lie. I *had* gone to the mall. And wandered around with nothing to do for about five hours.

"Oh yeah?" My mom arched her eyebrows. "Well, what about *during* school?"

Busted, I thought. I knew what she was going to say even before she said it.

"Kristin, Ms. McGuire called me at work to tell me that you skipped out on school when you were supposed to be delivering an announcement at some kind of assembly."

I could feel my face turning bright red. "Oh, um—um, yeah," I stammered. "I guess I sort of did do that."

"Sort of did that?" Mom sounded angrier by the second. "From what Ms. McGuire told me, I'd say you *definitely* did that. She was very concerned about you, Kristin. And frankly, so am I. And I just want to make it clear that this will never happen again. Understood?"

"Yes," I mumbled.

"Good. And just to be sure, I'm taking away your phone and television privileges for the next two weeks."

Two weeks? I guess skipping school was pretty bad, but two weeks seemed kind of harsh. I hadn't even skipped a whole day! Lacey manages to skip school all the time. Then again, according to her, her parents could pretty much care less where she is—as long as she isn't at home.

I trudged up to my room, my mother glaring after me. I couldn't blame her for being mad. I was even mad at myself. And I decided that Ms. McGuire had had a point this morning. Maybe I *couldn't* deal with the stress of being class president.

I decided I would face her first thing in the morning.

And resign.

Brian

"Lacey?"

"What do you want?" Lacey replied, sounding slightly irritated, which for Lacey is pretty much her regular phone voice.

"Hey. It's me, Brian," I said tentatively.

"Oh. Hi, Brian," she replied. She sounded even grumpier than her usual self.

I didn't comment on her lack of enthusiasm. It's usually better to be as nonconfrontational as possible when Lacey's in one of her moods. Besides, there was something important on my mind. It's not like I call Lacey Frells on a regular basis or anything.

"Did you ever hear from Kristin?" I asked hopefully.

"No," she replied. "I actually tried to call her tonight, but her mom said that she's grounded with no phone privileges for two weeks."

"Yeah," I said. "I got the same story."

"I bet it has to do with ditching that assembly today."

"Probably," I said. "That's kind of why I'm calling. Do you know why she skipped?"

"Oh, probably that whole Olympics Day drama." Lacey sounded bored.

"Wait," I said. "What do you mean?"

Lacey heaved a long sigh. "Oh, Kristin was all bent out of shape about this Olympics Day thing. She wanted the eighth grade to go on some dorky class trip, but the class council decided to do the Olympics Day instead. Kristin felt like her idea wasn't getting any respect. Didn't she tell you about it?"

"Not really," I said. "Kristin told me that she had a problem with the class council, but she never told me the details." Suddenly I remembered a flyer Blue had shown me this afternoon, advertising a sit-in against Olympics Day. Could Kristin have made it? It wasn't really like her to do something like that—unless she was really mad. I wondered if anyone had shown up for that protest. Everyone at the assembly seemed really jazzed for Olympics Day. . . .

"I don't get it," I said to Lacey. "What's wrong with Olympics Day?"

"I don't know—I guess the main problem was that Kristin liked her idea better. And you know she doesn't love sports and all that athletic junk. I mean, she digs cheerleading, but not running and that kind of thing. The Olympics Day thing was pure Bethel."

I knew that Kristin didn't like sports. She tended to roll her eyes and make gagging noises when Salvador and I talked about football or soccer. But even if she didn't understand why everyone else was so excited, it's not really like her to try to shoot down other people's ideas. In fact, that was one of the things I liked best about Kristin—she always stood behind other people and encouraged them.

"You know she's been feeling kind of insecure about student council since Ms. McGuire took over," Lacey said. "Maybe it was really important to her that everyone get behind her class-trip idea. And maybe when they didn't, she freaked out a little bit."

That sounded plausible. I know that Kristin can be a little insecure sometimes. And leave it to Lacey to figure it out. It's not like she's normally a supersensitive person . . . but I guess she can be, when it comes to people she cares about. "So what can we do?" I asked. "How can we make her feel better?"

"I'm probably not the best person to ask," Lacey replied. "I'm pretty sure she's mad at me right now."

"For what?" I asked.

Lacey sighed. "For harshing on her ideas like everyone else."

"What do you mean?"

"Don't ask. Let's just say that managing to say the wrong thing at the wrong time seems to be a piece of cake for me."

Poor Kristin, I thought. I couldn't believe she'd been going through this by herself. What kind of friends *were* we?

"Wait. I have an idea," Lacey suddenly announced.

Whatever it is, I thought, *it had better be a good one.*

Kristin

I had never dreaded going to school so much in my life.

"Good morning, Kristin," Ms. McGuire greeted me as I walked into her classroom. It was thirty minutes before the first bell—so I knew we'd have plenty of time to discuss the assembly. And my nonappearance.

"Good morning, Ms. McGuire," I said. "I hope I'm not disturbing you."

"Not at all." She gestured me to a desk across from where she was sitting. "I was actually hoping that I'd get a chance to talk to you."

I imagined that she was looking forward to kicking me out of office.

"Kristin, I know we discussed this briefly yesterday, and you assured me that you were capable of handling the job of class president. But that was before the assembly, which you did not attend."

"I know, Ms. McGuire," I responded. "And I apologize for missing the assembly. Maybe it *is* best if I step down from office."

Ms. McGuire actually looked shocked. Why was she so surprised? Wasn't this what she had wanted all along?

"Kristin." Ms. McGuire heaved a long sigh. "I don't want you to step down."

"You don't?" I asked. "But didn't you ask me to step down yesterday?"

"I asked you to consider handing over some of the responsibilities of the presidency if they were causing you too much stress," she corrected. "And if you feel that stepping aside is what's best for you, then by all means, that's what you should do. But I would prefer it if we could find a way to make the job less stressful for you. You're a good leader. You have the respect and admiration of your peers, and you're without a doubt the hardest-working student on the class council. You made the carnival a huge success, and I don't think there's anyone more deserving or capable of being class president."

What? Now I really couldn't believe my ears.

"You could use a little work on your organizational skills, but overall, you are a very good leader."

"Really?" I asked.

"Yes, Kristin, really," she answered. "But being class president does come with a lot of pressure. And if you do decide to remain in office, I'm not going to let up on you. I expect great things from you. Now with that said," Ms. McGuire continued, "I will still understand if you want to step down. You can have the day to think about it. But I'd like an answer from you by tomorrow morning whether you want to continue as president or not. And," she concluded, "if you do decide to remain president, you're going to have to refrain from pulling any stunts like skipping the assembly in the future. And whatever you decide to do, I expect you to give a formal apology to the student council at the next meeting."

"I understand." I nodded, swallowing the lump in my throat. "Thanks, Ms. McGuire." I got up from my seat. Even though I felt embarrassed about my recent behavior, I was also suddenly elated. Because suddenly I was sure that I wanted to remain class president more than anything. "I think I can give you that answer now. I will be the class president, but I'll also try hard to make sure that I share my responsibilities so that the pressure doesn't get to be too much. I think Bethel might be a big help in that area," I added, thinking out loud.

Ms. McGuire nodded. "Bethel is very organized, and she has a lot of great ideas. I think the two of you will work very well together."

"I know we will," I said warmly.

I turned to walk out the door. I was so relieved that Ms. McGuire was willing to give me another chance despite the way I'd been acting. I cringed as I thought of the attitude I'd been giving people lately—my friends, Ms. McGuire, Mrs. Bertram. It was about time I started setting everything right. With *everyone*.

"Oh, and Kristin?"

"Yes?" I turned back to Ms. McGuire, who was holding out a sheet of paper.

"Could you toss this in the recycling bin on your way out?" she asked.

I took the sheet out of her hands and turned it over so I could read the lettering on the front. It was the flyer I'd made for the sit-in. I looked up at Ms. McGuire. A tiny hint of a smile crossed her lips.

"No problem," I said, smiling back at her.

"So, we're ready to move past all this?" Ms. McGuire asked.

"Yes, we're definitely ready," I replied. And in my heart, I knew it was true.

By the time the first bell rang, I was practically walking on air. I found Mrs. Bertram and apologized for snapping at her the other day when she tried to talk to me about my paper. And she told me the paper had been really well written, even though I hadn't followed directions and I was still stuck with the D. She told me I still had a pretty decent grade in the class, though, so I knew I'd just have to work harder to pull myself back up to an A overall.

When lunchtime finally arrived, I couldn't wait to find Brian and tell him that everything was going to be okay. And I also couldn't wait to talk to Lacey. I felt like I should apologize to her for going off on her because of the attitude she had about my class-trip idea. I shouldn't have taken it so personally. Lacey was just being Lacey. Unlike me, she never cared much for student activities, whether they were my idea or someone else's.

And as I rounded the corner, there they were—Lacey and Brian, standing at my locker. I gave them a huge smile. "Hi, guys!"

I slipped my hand into Brian's, and he grinned sort of sheepishly. "Hey. Lacey and I have a surprise for you," he said, looking over at Lacey, who smiled at me.

I just stood there for a second, confused.

"Ahem." Lacey cleared her throat. I could tell that she was really excited about something, even though she was trying not to show it (in typical Lacey fashion). I lifted my eyebrows. "What?"

"Aren't you going to open your locker?" she asked.

I quickly dialed my combination and swung open the door. Six cupcakes, with little animals frosted on top, were nestled on top of my books.

"Where did these come from?" I asked, delighted.

"I made them for you last night," Lacey said.

"You . . . actually . . . baked?" I was in shock.

"Yeah, can you believe it?" Brian answered for her.

"Well, don't everybody make a big deal out of it," Lacey said irritably. "Anyone can get a box of Betty Crocker cake mix." She tried to flip her hair to the side to hide it, but I could see that she was suppressing a smile. "You didn't even notice the best part. Why don't you take a closer look at the cupcakes?"

I took one of the cupcakes out of my locker and squinted at it. And that's when I figured out that the animals frosted on the top weren't just any animals—they were mammoths. Like the mammoths you see at the La Brea Tar Pits.

"I used brown icing so it would look like tar," Lacey said proudly. "I know you were sad that people didn't go for your class-trip idea. So instead of taking you to the tar pits, which does not interest me *at all*"—Lacey wrinkled her nose—"I decided to bring the tar pits to *you*."

I felt my grin grow even wider. I knew Lacey must have gone to a lot of trouble to make these. And I couldn't remember her ever doing anything in the kitchen besides pouring herself a glass of water.

"They're beautiful." I took a bite out of the one I was holding. Mmmm. Vanilla with chocolate frosting—my favorite. "Oh, Lacey," I said. "This is the sweetest thing you've ever done!" I rushed to hug her.

"Okay, okay, don't get cupcake on my shirt," she said. Typical Lacey. Hard and crusty on the outside, warm and mushy on the inside.

"I'm serious," she went on. "If you get cupcake on me, I'll punch you."

Okay, warm and mushy on the inside—*sometimes*.

I was feeling overwhelmed by my emotions, so I decided I needed to change the subject. "So, what's going on with you guys?" I asked.

"Well, did I tell you about the big surfing competition I'm going to enter with Blue this weekend?" Brian asked.

"Surfing competition?" I repeated. "But you don't even surf!"

"I do now," Brian answered proudly. "Blue's been teaching me."

"That's great," I told him. "But are you really ready to enter a competition?"

"No," Brian answered. "No way! Are you crazy? But Blue says it's just for fun. It's not like we're going to try to win or anything. But I'm hoping I might win by the time we have the Olympics Day surfing competition!"

"What? Surfing's not an Olympic sport!" I said.

"That's why you'll be receiving my petition to make it one next week, Ms. President," he replied, bowing.

I laughed. "So when's the big surf-off?" I asked.

"This Saturday," Brian answered. "Do you guys wanna come?"

"Definitely," I replied without hesitating. I looked expectantly at Lacey.

Lacey snorted. "Surfing contest? I don't think so."

"So," Brian asked. "Is anyone else ready for lunch? I'm starved."

"Lunch? Who needs lunch?" I held up my cupcake. I really did have the best friends in the world. "I say, let them eat cake!"

Sweet Valley Surfing Competition Rules and Regulations

1. This is an amateur competition. No pros allowed.
2. There are two divisions in the men's tournament:
   > Under-eighteen boys;
   > Over-eighteen men.
3. Each heat will consist of four participants from the same division.
4. Heats will last twenty minutes.
5. Participants may make as many runs as possible during the twenty-minute heat.
6. Yield to surfers dropping in on peak of wave.
7. Surfers will be judged for each ride on a scale of 1 through 10, based on the following criteria:
   > Technique;
   > Wave selection;
   > Style;
   > Overall performance.
8. No smoking on the beach.
9. Absolutely no profanity.

Brian

"Don't worry, Brian, I know you'll do better in your next heat," Kristin encouraged me. She was rubbing extra sunblock on my shoulders, which were already turning pink. "You just need to relax."

I took a deep breath and tried to chill out, but it wasn't easy. I was in the middle of my first surfing competition with hundreds of people watching, and I had hardly learned to stand on my board. But it helped to have Kristin there, rubbing my shoulders. And it was especially nice to have her back to her old normal self. Jessica and Elizabeth Wakefield were there too, along with Salvador and Damon and Blue's brother, Leaf.

On my first heat I hadn't managed to stand up even once. But I didn't care. Like Blue and I had been saying all along, we were just doing it for fun. And so far, our day at the beach had been totally fun. I hadn't seen Perry, Leo, or Glenn all day, except from a distance, so I didn't have to listen to them heckling me.

Blue had been in Leo's heat at the beginning of the competition, and neither one of them did too well (Blue had a pretty spectacular wipeout on one of his rides, and Leo wiped out twice). I think Blue had barely beaten him in the scoring, but it didn't matter. Leo might have cared about the score, but Blue didn't.

And neither did I, really. I just wanted to stand up once and ride one wave, at least for five seconds or so.

"Hey, Brian," Salvador called out. "Isn't that Blue out there on the break?"

"Yeah, that's him," I answered. "Yo, Leaf! Check it out—it's your brother out there."

"He's lookin' pretty good," Leaf answered casually.

I watched Blue out in the water as he and the other three guys in his heat waited for the perfect wave. He duck dived through the first two waves and then got ready for the third. From where I was standing, it looked like a big one.

As the wave got close, I could see Blue getting ready to stand. As soon as it was just about under him, he stood up smoothly—in one fluid motion—and dropped in on the apex of the wave. He rode it perfectly, almost all the way to the shore. In the middle of his ride he raised his arms and flexed his muscles. He gave a big, goofy grin, and all of us cracked up. Then he fell off his board, and we all cheered as loud as we could.

"That was awesome!" Damon yelled.

"Hey, how come you can't surf like that, Damon?" Salvador teased.

Damon raked his hand through his dark hair. "I'm too tall," he said simply, but his eyes were smiling.

"I'm taller than you are," I pointed out. "And I've been surfing."

"I was talking about actually standing up and riding the wave," Salvador put in. "Not just paddling out there and falling off your board when the wave hits you."

I grinned at him. "You're just jealous of my incredible surfing ability," I said, and we both laughed.

Elizabeth picked up a handful of sand and watched it drain through her fingers. "I'd like to learn to surf," she said. "And I'd like to see you try it too, Sal."

Salvador looked over the top of his shades. "I'm a lover, not a surfer," he said in a suave voice.

"Yeah, right," Elizabeth said, and threw a clump of wet sand at him.

It hit him on the shoulder. "Watch it!" he complained. "You're messing up my super-smooth image!"

"Spare us, El Salvador," Jessica said, reaching into the cooler we'd brought for soda.

I turned back to Salvador. "Seriously, why don't you give it a try?"

"Nah, I don't think so." Salvador brushed the sand off his arm. "You're the brave one."

Blue suddenly appeared on the beach in front of us, walking across the sand with his board under his arm. "Hey, guys, did you see that last run? Was that awesome or what?"

"It was great," Leaf said proudly.

"Yeah," Damon agreed, "even if you do say so yourself."

Blue pointed out at the water. "Hey, Brian, I think your final heat is about to start."

"All right." I grabbed Leaf's board and walked toward the surf. Suddenly my stomach filled with butterflies.

"You can do it, Brian!" Kristin called after me. I got to the water and was about to paddle out when I noticed Glenn and Leo right there with me. Were they in my heat? Suddenly the butterflies got a whole lot worse.

"Hey, Brian, what are you doing here?" Leo taunted, splashing in beside Glenn. "I thought this heat was for people who actually know how to surf."

"Yeah, dude. I think the girls' tournament is

in a couple of weeks," Glenn added, running his fingers through his damp hair. "Maybe you should wait for that."

That comment really annoyed me. *I'd rather be in the girls' tournament,* I thought. For one thing, the girls I'd seen surfing while Blue and I were practicing over the past few days were really good. Most of them could dust Leo and Glenn without even thinking about it. And for another thing, I was pretty sure the girls weren't jerks.

But like it or not, I was stuck in this heat with these guys. I just ignored them and started paddling out toward the break.

When I got there, I swam up next to Leo and Glenn and some other kid, and we all waited patiently for a decent wave. I duck dived through the first couple of waves and felt happy I could do that without falling off my board. Then I saw a big one coming. As it got closer, I braced myself.

When I thought the apex was beneath me, I stood up on my board—in one fluid motion. For a moment my heart dropped—I was going to ride the wave! My feet floundered as I tried to find the sweet spot . . . and couldn't. I must have been too far forward because the back of the board suddenly popped up behind me, and I did a nosedive . . . straight down. I plunged face first into the ocean, water swirling all around me. The waves pummeled me as I got churned around in the water until I couldn't even tell which way was up.

But I remembered what Blue had taught me and didn't panic. When my toe touched the sand, I shot straight up to the top of the water. I pulled on my leash until I got a hold on my board. Then I scrambled back onto it.

I looked across the water at the beach and saw my group of friends laughing and cheering. Salvador was clapping and whistling, and Kristin was jumping up and down. I looked around for Glenn and Leo and finally noticed them riding their waves in toward shore.

So I hadn't managed to stand up after all. And they had. Oh, well.

Next time.

When I walked across the beach toward Blue and my other friends, everyone was hooting and hollering my name.

"Way to go, Brian," Leaf yelled. "That was an awesome wipeout! The best one in the entire competition."

"Yeah, Brian, nice going," Blue added. "See? It totally doesn't matter if you lose or even if you get up on your board. Surfing's a blast no matter what."

"Well, Leo and Glenn made it up on their boards," I answered.

"Yeah, but that other guy won the heat," Blue pointed out. "So who cares?"

"Look at them over there." Sal pointed over at Leo, Glenn, and Perry, sitting by themselves on the sand. "They don't even have a cheering section."

I looked around at my own little cheering section, including my number-one cheerleader, Kristin, and my friend Blue. Even though I hadn't managed to stand up on my board, I couldn't help feeling really, really good.

"Hey, Blue, don't you have another heat coming up?" I asked.

"Yeah, but I think I'm going to skip it," he answered with a shrug. "You're done with all your heats, and I just had my best ride of the day. I might as well quit while I'm ahead. Anyway, I'm starving," he said, breaking into a grin. "So what do you say, Leaf? Pizza party at our house?"

"Pizza party it is," Leaf answered with a big smile. "And by the way, Gnarler is ready for a test run if anyone's interested."

"All right!" I cried. "First dibs!"

"Finally, a surfing competition you can win," Salvador teased.

I grinned at him. "You said it." But as I looked around at Blue and Leaf, and Kristin and the rest of my friends, I had to admit, I didn't really care about the game all that much.

I felt like I'd already won.

Check out the **all-new** ....

(Sweet Valley Web site—)

www.sweetvalley.com

New Features

Cool Prizes

The *ONLY* official Web site!

Hot Links

(And much more!)

Francine Pascal's

SWEET VALLEY jr. high

You hate your **alarm clock.**

You hate your **clothes.**

You're going to love Jr. High.